ONE OF 1500 LIMITED EDITION COPIES

ONE DAY ALL THIS WILL BE YOURS

ADRIAN TCHAIKOVSKY

SOLARIS

First published 2021 by Solaris
an imprint of Rebellion Publishing Ltd,
Riverside House, Osney Mead,
Oxford, OX2 0ES, UK

www.solarisbooks.com

ISBN: 978-1-78108-874-6

10 9 8 7 6 5 4 3 2 1

A CIP catalogue record for this book is available from
the British Library.

Designed & typeset by Rebellion Publishing

Printed in the UK

ONE DAY ALL THIS WILL BE YOURS

CHAPTER ONE

ANOTHER PERFECT DAY at the end of the world.

I'm up with the sun, as usual. Not a cloud in the sky. And if there was, it'd still be a perfect day because, when you're a farmer-type like I am, then rain's good too, in its proper place and time. And I cheat, of course; I have some top-grade weather satellites invisibly overhead, governed by a computer system that's smart enough to bluff me at poker, let alone beat me at chess. Rain when I need it, sun when I don't. Snow when I decide it's midwinter. How I love the rugged outdoors life! Living out here with nothing but the fields and the animals and literally the best technological support that anyone ever invented.

I wasn't always a farmer. I've had to learn the hard way, mostly by struggling through impenetrable user manuals—

Welcome new owner of the Kinhardy-Wollop Robotic Threshalot Model 94! Even with all the time in the world at my disposal I wasn't sure I'd get it all going at first. But it turns out that if you yank on your own bootstraps enough there's no limit to how much of a good thing you can get going. The place basically runs itself. The place literally *does* run itself.

Two decades, it took me, tugging on those bootstraps. Worth every moment. And every moment I spent on it, even when I was sleeping under the stars and going back in time to raid food banks for dinner, I was telling myself how much better off I was than during the fighting. I'm not doing that again. This soldier boy's retired to the country.

I mean, let's face it. *Nobody's* doing that again. World peace, man. Forever and forever.

I spend half the morning with the tractor. It's a new model I picked up a month ago, rusting in a Soviet barn back in nineteen sixty-two. I'm not lauding this as the pinnacle of agricultural technology, never to be surpassed. But restoring the old girl has kept me busy for a few weeks, and it's good to have a hobby. And I've had to make some changes to its energy pathways because I don't want to have to go raid the fossil fuels of the past every three days, nor set up my own refining industry here. So, magic tractor, basically.

Like I say, I do cheat. Cheating makes life easier and I'm all about that easy life.

You've heard about the magic tractor, right? Went round the corner and turned into a field. And when I get the intractable machine working and potter off to where the rice paddies are I tell myself that good old joke again and my voice rings out across the rolling fields and as far as the horizon without ever having to encounter another human being.

They're harvesting the wheat and the corn as I drive past in my Soviet Speedster with its spanking new coat of red paint. No heads bob up to see what I'm laughing about; there are no heads to bob. There have been maybe three moments in history when agricultural automation reached absolutely perfect efficiency. I have pillaged those moments, brought the goodies back here and spent many happy days trying to get their incompatible systems to talk to one another. Like clockwork, now. Planting, tending, harvesting, storing, all accomplished by a fleet of machines from the size of a house to the size of a gnat. Meaning I get to renovate antiquated agricultural vehicles from the twentieth century and drive about with a straw hat on and a wisp of grass in the corner of my mouth like a proper yokel.

Out where the flocks are, for an audience of precisely one robot sheepdog, I practice the banjo. I am still, I am delighted to find, terrible at it. It's no fun to pick up skills too fast, not when you're a man of leisure with all the time in the world.

Literally all the time. My time; my world.

Feeding time for Miffly next. I love to watch her bound out from where she's been hiding, already salivating *à la* Pavlov at the sound of the bell I've struck. As she slobbers over her repast, I chow down on a ham and pickle sandwich which tastes all the better knowing it's my ham and my pickles. I could get by with a much smaller operation if

I'd just be happy eating the same thing over and over, but you go enough years on ration kits and you relish a little variety in your diet. This year I'm going to put in a salmon run, I decide, really push the boat out, which will mean getting a boat. I'll have to go back to some point when there were still salmon, and read up on what you even do with one. I have a feeling they're one of those species with a ludicrously inconvenient life cycle, up into far highland lakes and then all the way to the sea, that kind of pointless nonsense. Which suggests I'm setting myself up for a major project that'll keep me happily busy for years.

With evening drawing on I potter back to the house in the Speedster. She's still not running entirely satisfactorily—engine sounding a bit grumbly—and that, too, is good. Means I get to open the hood and tinker again. Because one of the best things you can do, if you've actually achieved perfection, is introduce the imperfect, just to keep things interesting.

Miffly wants to come with me, of course. She discovers sudden bursts of affection after being fed. She trails the tractor all the way to the house with a hopeful look on her face and then wants to come inside like she used to when she was little. I can't really have her scratching the chair legs any more, though, so I politely but firmly close the door on her whining and turn in with the sense of a day well spent.

The next morning, the alarms go off.

It's been a while since they did. You always think each time is going to be the last. I check the satellite map and see something's turned up in the middle of the barley. Radiation and heavy metal counts suggest that crop is going to end up shot into the sun to stop a lot of nastiness getting into the food chain (which is to say, me). But this is part of the price of perfection, and I don't complain too much to myself. No time for the nice fry-up I was hoping for, though, so I neck a cup of strong coffee and then hop on the Speedster, crunching the buttered heel of yesterday's loaf. While the robots harvest the grain and churn the butter, I bake the bread myself. I do good bread, if I say so myself.

Out in the barley, I spot the *something* soon enough. Hard to miss a cratered circle of dead plant life a hundred metres across. The actual intrusion's relatively small. Just a capsule half again the size of a man, so that I wonder if it's nothing but electronics inside. It looks rough, to be honest. My tractor is decidedly more aesthetically pleasing, for all that I'm looking at the pinnacle of a technology centuries in advance of the flower of Communism.

Even as I'm driving over, thinking about soil decontamination measures and just how much I'm going to have to replace, a hatch springs open and a man falls out. He ends up on hands and knees, smoking slightly, wearing a suit of plastic and foil that's still cabled and ducted into the capsule he came from. He's coughing. Actually he's vomiting. Rough trip, I decide charitably, although he looks as though endemic health problems are also a factor. His face is as hollow as a famine victim's, unshaven, skin rugged with spots and surgery scars and a couple of melanomas.

I jump down off the Speedster and run over the dying barley to him. "Hello!" in English, Mandarin, Russian (newly fluent after the work on the tractor), Spanish and Croatian.

I stop three metres away. We stare at each other. After a moment he starts crying. Between sobs he chokes out a question, and on the third repetition my translation software pegs it as a blend of Arabic and a cocktail of romance languages and I can make myself understood.

"That's right," I tell his tears. "You made it. Welcome to the end times."

His name is Rigo. He can't really say much at first; too overwhelmed. I just sit with him as he fumbles in his clumsy gloves with all the homemade-looking equipment on his capsule. It's such a botch-job in there I can't even see what he's trying to do, except it isn't doing what he wants. At last he sits down again, still crying. "It's broken," he tells me.

"What's that?"

"Rad counter. Not getting a reading."

I laugh. Rigo's blank stare suggests he's not used to people laughing, possibly at all.

"The only radiation here's background, friend." In fact the main source of radiation is him, but no sense bringing him down. I introduce myself instead, offer to shake his hand except he doesn't know that custom. Poor guy looks shell-shocked.

"Deep breaths," I counsel. He's reacting to everything: the sky, the fields, the horizon. I'm guessing where he comes from the Great Outdoors ain't so great anymore.

I coax him onto the Speedster and take him back to the house. By the time we arrive I've worked out robots don't freak him out, but animals do, from the sheep to the smallest insects. Miffly doesn't put in an appearance and that's likely just as well for Rigo's mental health. Best to break things to people gently.

I make a bit of a spread, at the house. Rigo sits at the rough wooden table, still in his suit with its scatter of disconnected hoses. Unshaven, pockmarked, twitchy. And yet it's starting to get through to the poor guy that he's actually done it. He probably thought he'd just die, when they sent him off in that tiny capsule: he's one of the desperate ones. The moment it dawns on them that, yes, this is the promised land, the idyllic future where the world is healed and everything's good—I still love it. Seeing that lifelong tension slowly inch out of his limbs. Handing him a plate with a cold leg of chicken and some crisp tomatoes, hard-boiled egg and some of that pear chutney I made last year that turned out extra-well. Food is one of those things in life that really repays putting an effort in.

The house is based on a nineteenth-century French farmhouse I saw once and rather liked. Didn't have the chance to really enjoy it at the time, what with the war on and the Causality Bombs and all—had to get out of the whole region double time—but I remembered. And, afterwards, I went back and found it, and had a replica built here, updated for all mod cons in such a way that none of it shows. Rustic simplicity backed by the absolute best in smart home systems.

"Tell me what it's like, where you come from," I prompt Rigo. He's been alternating between eating and staring out of the window and crying some more. Overwhelmed; a little conversation about his home will ground him.

And it's a grim story. He lives underground with a few thousand other survivors in the throes of a nuclear winter. He's third generation, and it's getting worse for him and his. The bunker leadership are doing their level best to control everyone's thoughts and kid them that it's all going swell, but by the time Rigo reaches majority, even that's fallen over and they know they're all screwed. And maybe if they'd just settled down to smell the irradiated roses, concentrate on the near-end of Maslow's Hierarchy of Needs, then they'd be a little more stable. All their effort has been going into their science team, though. Their leaders are a technical elite who believe they can rewind the apocalypse, or at least open a door they can all escape through.

The floodgates are open, now; Rigo just can't stop talking, like he's never been able to express any of this before because he's lived cheek by jowl with people for whom it was all old news. I'm the only appreciative audience he's ever had.

Rigo's life has been rubbish, frankly. I nod and sip my coffee sympathetically. I remember what it was like, at the height of the war, and I reckon Rigo's whole life has been like that. A litany of failing systems, sickness, hunger, brutality and oppression. He volunteered as an experimental subject because it would get his family more food. He expected a death sentence. He doesn't even know if the experiment was supposed to bring him here. He doesn't even know where *here* is.

"The end times," I explain gently. "The postepochalypse."

Blank looks from Rigo.

By now I know fairly precisely when he's from. Rigo's

a survivor of the war before the last one. I don't want to tell him that, no matter how crap his life is, back home, people are going to work themselves back into a position for one more great war before things settle down to the life I'm enjoying. One more War To End All Wars, only this time it really will. That's *my* war, of course. Rigo was born around a century before it broke out. That's how long it took people to put the world back together enough for it to be worth breaking into pieces again.

I get the wine out, later. I do have some vineyards of my own but, of all my agricultural experiments, that one has not yet produced anything I'd be happy sharing. Instead I tend to go on sporadic shopping expeditions to particularly good years in France and Australia and California, and then leave the bottles to mature in some secluded corner of history before retrieving them for the cellar.

"Your very good health," I toast Rigo, although that ship has fairly obviously sailed.

As he drinks, and cries some more at just how beautiful it all is, how not-underground and not-radioactive, I load the plates into the dishwasher and ring the bell.

After he's drained his wine, Rigo stands decisively.

"I have to get back," he tells me. "They need to know." He blinks back more tears. "This place... we're saved. We're actually saved." He's lived his whole life in the certain knowledge that he's going to die young, and that the next generation will die younger, and probably there won't be a generation after that at all. And now he's spent a day at the farm and knows things will get better.

When we go outside, I introduce him to Miffly.

I don't think he has the necessary frame of reference to recognise her. I don't think palaeontology is a big part of the curriculum in his time. All he sees is *big* and *teeth* and *ravaging*. And fluff, of course, because like most therapod dinosaurs Miffly is just a great fuzzball of feathers. I know I'm biased but, she is ridiculously adorable when she's not actually eating people.

Rigo doesn't get much more crying time in, because I haven't fed Miffly since yesterday and because she knows full well what that bell means.

While she's picking the tinfoil out of her teeth I go to the big barn, because now I've got work to do. It's the price of perfection, really; sometimes you've got to get your hands dirty. I go past the Soviet Speedster and the gyrocopter and the hovertank, all my little hobby projects, until I get to the armillary sphere that is *my* time machine. Army surplus, of course, but then I'm all the army there is left and *everything* is surplus.

Between our little chat and my instruments' examination of his capsule, I have a fairly exact idea of Rigo's point of departure, so it's easy enough to set the machine to head back there. Rigo's capsule, by the way, wouldn't have made the return trip, or that was my system's assessment. A miracle he managed the one way, to be honest. Most likely the labs that sent him would never strike lucky again, but I can't really take the chance.

I go back to that cramped, irradiated, skyless place, thronging with filthy, hungry, desperate people. Reeking of sickness. Eating itself. I have lived like that. It's not as though I'm not sympathetic. But no. No exceptions. Or where would it end?

I go back further, twenty years or so. That's the trick, really. No point killing the dictator when the zeitgeist that produced him would just throw up another. Go back and kill the zeitgeist, and the dictators will look after themselves. I make sure a select handful of scientific minds are never born. I sabotage a few systems. To be honest I wonder if I shouldn't just wipe out the whole bunker a generation early; honestly, it might be kinder that way. It's not necessary, though. I prefer the light touch. And when I'm done, I have utterly destroyed that culture's capacity for travelling in time. They will live and they will die and they will never leave the period they were luckless enough to be born into. And they will never trouble the glorious solitude of my farm.

After that it's home and bed, that quintessential farmer's feeling of being tired after a day well spent in toil. One more perfect day at the end of the world.

CHAPTER TWO

THEY ALL COME here in the end.

I mean, it isn't exactly a full time job, destroying people's dreams of time travel, but it's busier work than you'd imagine. You might think that historical opportunities for the invention of a time machine are fairly limited, but that's only because I'm so rigorous about my self-appointed job. That unfortunate you heard about, down your street, or maybe two streets away: the one whose house went up in the gas explosion, or who went under a bus? That could have been my doing. There might have been a prototype time machine in their cellar, cobbled together out of soap bottles and double-sided tape. Or perhaps a descendent of theirs might have had a revelation about the nature of four-dimensional space that would have revolutionised science forever, if only they'd survived long enough to have any descendants. Or else it was just something else about them that would tip the scales, lead inexorably to a future where some other bright spark, less easily erased, would have the Big Idea. Perhaps the young jock I just pushed under a train would be the office bully who'd inspire some introvert genius to quit the day job and go invent time travel.

There, doesn't sound so bad that I killed him now, does it?

I'm not saying I feel good about Rigo, but the thing about rules is, they're there to be followed, no exceptions. And it's all in a good cause. Or it was originally all for the very best of causes, but now, I will admit, mission creep has set in. Because I have come to value my solitude, here at the postepochalyptic end of time. I don't mind visitors, but I make sure they don't stay long and, simultaneously, never leave. And I make sure nobody can ever come looking for them.

It's a calling. Or, if it's not a calling, then at least it's a vocation. Or, failing that, you have to have a hobby, don't you?

The last one, the one before Rigo, was one of my favourites. Turned up in his goggles and his leather jacket, great big waxed handlebar moustache. His machine was beautiful. I still have it—well, all right, I still have all of them, in the big hangar where I put the surplus time machines, but this one gets pride of place in the collection. Mahogany and teak, polished to a shine, and all the mountings gleaming brass. And steam! Steam and cogwheels and little things that light up or piston up and down or… It was like a toy store in the holidays, when he set all those moving parts going. I had him show me three times, just so I could do it myself after I'd got rid of him. I still set the thing in motion sometimes.

Hieronymus Blaylock, that was the name. The Honourable Professor Hieronymus Blaylock. Magnificent, a name as fancy as the moustache, as fancy as the machine he pitched up in. Knew his wine, beat me at chess, talked nineteen to the dozen about the spirit of human science. Took me the devil's own job to work out that he had actually set out from his own estates in Kent in 1911. There was a steampunk convention somewhere in 2008 that had a very near miss, believe you me. And when he saw Miffly! I swear his eyes lit up like it was Victoria's jubilee. "I say!" he said. "A real living *Tyrannosaurus*!" Because he *understood*, do you see, that exotic pets is basically one of the real justifications for having access to time travel. And I had to correct him, and explain that while *T. rex* is definitely one of the great iconic dinosaurs, for the purposes of eating people it's severely suboptimal because, frankly, we're far too small compared to its typical prey animals. Honestly, I've tried it; they're just not interested in us. They'd be picking little human bones out of their teeth for days, and with those tiny arms that's more trouble than it's worth.

Whereas the *Allosaurus*, on the other hand, is decidedly closer to our scale. Still terrifyingly big, but a damn sight nippier and far more amenable to a human-sized snack. And Hieronymus nodded as he digested this titbit of information, and then Miffly nodded as she digested him, and equilibrium was restored. And there was a mysterious explosion on a country estate in Kent in 1905, but nobody really noticed anything amiss because the owner was a notorious eccentric known for exploding things. Because I'm sentimental, and had rather liked Hieronymus, I exploded him on the exact same day that *T. rex* was formally named, to commemorate his mistake. But that's me all over, you see. I offer a bespoke service.

They all end up here, because this is the end-time. This is all the time there is. This is the trailing edge of what comes later, after the breach in regular transmissions left by the war. A bottleneck, you understand. You want to fling yourself forwards past the badlands of the war, this is where you end up. And I'll be waiting for you. Nobody gets by me. I have literally all the technology in the world, culled from every moment that anyone ever had a Big Idea, to make sure of exactly that. I am the ultimate surveillance state.

Before Hieronymus there was that scientist woman, Doctor Amari Amarylis, come from the twenty-first century because she wanted to get a jump on the scientific developments the future held in store. Something that might save her overburdened, climate-beset and politically unstable world. Very philanthropic, was our Doctor Amarylis. I genuinely think that, if I'd said, *I'll send the appropriate secrets back in a plain envelope if you agree to be devoured by Miffly,* she'd have said yes and made the ultimate sacrifice. I could have done it, too. It wouldn't have inconvenienced me at all. She wouldn't have understood that, though. She'd have been suspicious and asked the pertinent question: *Aren't you worried that would change things for you?*

And I'd have had to tell her. She was smart, and I'm not

really a good liar when you turn the spotlight on me. I'd have had to say, *No, because there's literally nothing you can do in your time that will change any epoch that comes after you, most certainly not this one. This is how it's going to be.* And that would have been cruel. That would have implied she couldn't save the world. Because she couldn't save the world, not the world she knew. Maybe make her own epoch a little better, but not stop everything coming down. I know. I know more than anyone.

And in the end there just seemed to be too much social awkwardness in making the offer, so I quietly shot her and buried her out in the fields—Miffly had already been fed, you see. Then I went back in my wartime time machine and hooked her mum up with the heir to a biscuit manufacturer millionaire before she met Doc Amarylis's dad, because I was feeling creative.

And before her it was the damn Greeks. You could have knocked me down with a bloody feather, seeing them. Three old guys with big beards turning up half-naked and half in bedsheets, with nothing but a very complicated diagram and something like a supercharged Antikythera mechanism. You've heard of that, right? You didn't know it was meant to be a time machine, right? And I'm not talking ancient aliens here. I mean there was going to be a school of Greek philosophy that would crack time travel back when Christ was still in short trousers. The things you don't expect, honestly. But there they were, three learned Athenian gentlemen half plastered on bad wine, gabbling away all at the same time. Took me four days of their riotous company to work out where and when they'd actually set off from. And I had a lot of cleaning up to do, after those guys. I don't mean the actual bodies, because there's a robot that mucks out Miffly's den. I had to trash an entire school of philosophical thought, though, starting four centuries before our three boys even began considering the nature of time. When I'd finished with my remedial work, an awful lot of things they taught you in the history books had become collateral damage, up to and including Alexander the Great, Plato and, to the great joy of schoolchildren everywhere, trigonometry. And it didn't matter, because nothing does any more. Because of the war.

That was my big idea, at the start. When the dust had settled and I looked around and realised that it was just me. That, despite never wanting it, I'd been left in possession of the field, and the field was human history, for what that was now worth.

Peace in our time, I thought. We actually had peace, world peace—that thing everyone says they want, and nobody lifts a finger to actually make happen. Peace, blessed peace, had finally descended. And who better to appreciate it but me, the war veteran, who'd spent the majority of his adult life fighting? Who'd lost so much—literally everything, in fact? Who'd come through the War To End All Wars? Peace, and I'd damn well better appreciate it, because there was literally nobody else left to appreciate it for me, and its not exactly a job you can devolve to a robot. Post-war, and I knew then and there that I must never allow such a terrible thing to happen again.

CHAPTER THREE

NOBODY KNOWS WHERE they were when the Causality War started.

It arose out of a regular war; nobody's going to kick off by using their ultimate sanction, after all. It started small, in fact. Some territorial... or else it was a resource war, or... I'd say I forget, but that's not entirely fair on me. I lived through it, after all. I was there cheering them on, or possibly shaking my head and *tsk*ing between my teeth, when the announcement was made. I signed up and/or was conscripted into the army. What did you do in the Causality War, Daddy? I fought, son. And in retrospect, that is the only thing that I can say with any certainty.

Some small business between some small combatants, a proxy war because our proxy had always had it in for their proxy, or vice versa, and at some point we got so invested in backing our proxy, and they theirs, that *we* were just fighting *them* and the proxies had become nothing more than ground zero for a war that expanded out across the globe.

And it eats me up, that I can't even tell you what it was for. I mean, I guess what it was for was that we knew there was going to have to be a war and they knew there was going to have to be a war, and then some local nonsense sparked off that we and they agreed was a good enough excuse to get it out of our systems. But I don't know who the proxies were or what it was about each other that they couldn't live with, and I don't know why their little war became *our* Big War that became the Causality War. I *can't* know these things. Nobody can. Nobody ever will, any more. There is no archaeologist to excavate some site giving vital insights into the origins of the conflict. No godlike aliens will come down and reconstruct those tumultuous days. It's gone.

I don't know with what weapons World War III will be fought, Al Einstein said, *but the war after that will be fought with sticks and stones*. Except that turns out to be almost exactly wrong, if the weapons the next war is fought with are time machines. And I have said that to his face, and you'd think of all bloody people that Einstein would understand, might even have some answers. But, after listening to enough of what I had to say, he just ended up crying on the pavement, stuck it out at the patent office and never went on to work out relativity, so I guess I'm on my own as far as the theory side of things goes.

People have described a lot of things as an ultimate

weapon, a doomsday measure, a holiday at the final resort. None of them were, not really. Even nukes are just a better way of killing people that leaves a longer-lasting stain on the carpet. City-devouring intercontinental missiles and orbital railgun strikes: these things are on a straight line of development from slings and thrown rocks. But time machines really are the ultimate sanction. And just like the nukes of an earlier era, by the time the war started, everyone had them, and everyone had signed a lot of important pieces of paper swearing they wouldn't use them. Because we knew that as soon as anyone actually *used* a time machine with hostile intent, that would be it.

And we knew whoever used them first would theoretically have an insuperable advantage.

Think about it. You're there in the heat of a war that's only getting hotter. Hundreds of thousands of people just died in some city you were probably quite fond of. Millions of people are dead on your side. Millions of people are dead on their side. Tens of millions of people who probably didn't much identify with either side are also dead, because they made the foolish mistake of being within five thousand miles of some manner of strategic objective. And, gathering dust in the shed, you have a fleet of time machines that you have made the very pinkiest swear *not to use under any circumstances*. What do you do?

And it's easy to characterise that fateful decision-maker as desperate or greedy or a fanatic—a monster of some stripe or flavour—but it didn't have to be like that. It's not all about going back and killing someone's parents, take it from me. What if you could send an agent discreetly back to a year before the war started and defuse the tensions that led to the war? What if you could put a word in someone's ear that meant the two proxies were never at each others' throats anyway? What if you could make *us* and *them* firm friends a century before, heal the divide before it occurred? What if you could nudge history a whole millennium earlier so that the whole ideological basis of the enemy just never came into being, and everyone happily ended up more like you without ever knowing that it might have been different? What if you could go back *two* thousand years and introduce an egalitarian participatory government without all that tedious round of kings and queens that went on for so long and accomplished so little? Wouldn't the thanks you'd get from generations of schoolchildren alone make it worth the effort?

And if you did it *now*, right now, before your opposite number did it, then there would literally be no comeback. No fallout, no retaliatory launch. You go and change history so that there's no war, and they can never do it to you. But if you stick by those agreements you signed while *they* give in to temptation, then it's *your* history getting changed and it's *you* who can never retaliate or complain, or even know that a moment ago you were in the middle of a war.

And both *you* and *they* are looking at the big red button on your executive desk that says 'launch time machines,' and looking at the casualty figures, the appalling cost of the conflict, the generations of ruin you've wrought on the world. And you have at your theoretical disposal a Final

Word unlike any other in history. Because, unlike nukes, it doesn't even make a mess. It cleans up not only after itself but *before* itself as well. It makes the mess *never have happened*. You're not only ending the war, you're literally saving lives. All those people *won't have died* after all! Sending in the time squads won't even be an act of war, it'll be an act of *un-war*.

And so you do it, and maybe you do it a moment before *they* do, and a moment before is all that's needed, in time travel. Except that, quite possibly unknown to you, both you and they already went back in time. Not to do anything. Not to change things. In the same way that, in peacetime, you do your level best to seed *their* country with agents as a purely contingent measure, just in case they're up to something. The past is another country, and this is one thing they do there that's exactly the same. Your security agencies had people secretly scattered back through history, and their agencies did too. Just in case anyone got to the point where all those agreements not to use time machines became too onerous. As, of course, they did.

So you sent your time soldiers back to dismantle the cause of the war, and quite possibly the cause of the enemy, to make your present a more amenable time where everyone wasn't killing everyone else and where everyone, moreover, thought and acted and believed a lot more like you—for surely that was *better* than the whole bloody war business. And their agents already back in time reported back to an HQ that no longer existed in a country that wasn't their own any more, quite possibly (depending on how far you went back) even speaking a different language. And so they turned straight round and went back to either restore the motherland they remembered or to screw you over, depending on the balance between patriotism and vengeance in any individual agent's mind. And the next day your own time agents checked in at your office and found the wrong faces on the money and the wrong backside on the presidential chair, and that tigers weren't extinct but elephants were—again, depending on how far anyone went back to change things. And so they went back to make their own defensive or offensive alterations to history. And, for good measure, they mobilised everyone else who had a time machine and gave them marching orders. And some of those mobilised people didn't even remember the time and place they were working to restore, they just had a hacked chain of command and some rather rose-tinted ideas of how things *should* be. And maybe your first order of business was to go back and remove the other side's capability to build, invent or even generally *conceive* of time machines, but that doesn't work, because those time machines already in operation in the past don't just vanish. They get orphaned instead, products of a sequence of events that never happened. And so they go back and try to restore their own timeline, just as you did, and most likely all they have of that timeline is unreliable memory and some wiki articles still stored in the memory of their phones. Or not even that. There's no hard line between things turning out how they were supposed to be and things turning out how you'd prefer them to have been.

This is how we fought the Causality War. A war where you never saw soldiers from the other side, not because you were launching high tech projectiles at each other from ridiculous distances, but because you almost never occupied a common frame of reference. The weapons you launched at each other were cascading chains of historical events, and each one simultaneously hit and caused colossal collateral damage, and did no damage at all, because what was left in its wake was a happy smiling world with no idea there was a war on.

Killing Rigo has left me feeling oddly lonely, here at the end of the world. It happens every so often, usually after I've removed another threat to the continuum. Most of the time the solitude is a plus on the ledger, but every so often I actually end up liking one of Miffly's aperitifs. I remember what it was like when there were other people to share a world with, and when your mission is most definitely to be the last man standing, that can be a problem. Thankfully there's a whole world of company just a step away. One little trip and I can gatecrash any party I choose, take in a show, join an expedition, hobnob with any wits and bon vivants I choose. And be back in time for tea, no matter how long a holiday I just took, because time travel.

Time travel, frankly, is aces. If it hadn't been co-opted as the ultimate weapon, just think of how much fun people could have had. I've thought about it: people could have had zero fun with it. The problem with time travel is that it's the ultimate weapon whether you intend to use it that way or not. I do wonder whether the way things turned out after the Causality War was inevitable the moment someone invented the first time machine (and the problem with someone inventing the first time machine is that someone else immediately took a trip to ten years before and invented the *first* first time machine so they could grab the patent, and so on, and so on).

Right now, though, I feel in the mood for a show, and it so happens there's a performance of *Two Gentlemen of Verona* where Will Kempe is in spectacular form, and so I head off there, standing in the crowd under a light drizzle while the funnyman goes through his rib-tickling paces. Not exactly the piece of Shakespeare you'd think would stick in the memory, but the thing about theatre is that live performance is everything and Kempe is a master of comic timing. Far better than watching Dick Burbage chew the scenery through *Hamlet*, believe me.

And it's a good show. It's just as I remember it, which in itself is reassuring because it's literally the same performance and any changes would indicate some active time agent I've somehow overlooked. And yet I'm never one hundred per cent comfortable, watching the players strut and fret their hour upon the stage. My eyes keep drifting across the mob of groundlings, across the posh crowd in their expensive seats. I'm looking for familiar faces, whether I want to or not. Just instinct, really. There's nobody left of the old crowd, but that doesn't stop me hunting them out.

The time before last when I came to this show, I spotted one of the final few, and took the appropriate sanctions— meaning, I went out to the car park and trashed their time machine so when they tried to make their timely departure from the stage, there was no exit for them to take. And then the scene ended, and so did they.

And that end is coming up. It's the most frustrating thing about this particular show: the curtain comes down before Kempe's finished, and I have to be gone before it does or it's my curtain call too. I hear the last joke, but never the punchline. And Kempe's a master improviser, too, so it's not as though I can just grab the *Collected Works* and see how it turned out.

But at least there are no old friends in the audience any more. Or old foes.

Friends, foes: after enough back and forth in the war, I realised the difference was less than academic. There must have been a moment of revelation, but if so, it's been erased with everything else. A moment when I met someone wearing the wrong hat for the period, using a model of mobile phone that probably hadn't been in circulation back in the court of Prester John. A moment when we looked at each other and gave half-hearted code words and countersigns that nobody else could know because they were the product of a chain of events that didn't exist any more. A moment when I realised the distinction of *us* and *them* had been abraded away because everybody's motherland had gone through so many visions and revisions that we were all chronological bastards.

For me, that was the breaking point in the war. To understand that the conflict now consisted solely of soldiers doing a duty owed to a non-existent nation—or faction, or corporation. Doing what they thought they were supposed to do, what they vaguely remembered was their mission, what they'd reinterpreted as the right thing. And the problem is, with time travel, there *is* no right thing. There is a multiplicity of wrong things, and you can shove your hand in the box and see which one you draw out. All those stories and films where someone has a time machine and they're going back to restore their own timeline? That's like a blindfolded archer who's been spun around a thousand times loosing an arrow and hitting the exact bull's eye on a target someone removed the day before. You screwed it when you stood on the butterfly effect, and just stamping on more random insects isn't ever going to bring back the precise chain of events that leads to the world you came from.

And yet we were all trying. Hundreds of dedicated time warriors leaping about like fleas on the back of history, trying to win the war. And sometimes I met people who also understood that the war could only be lost, but they still wanted it to be lost *their way*. Every alliance between us failed, because whatever goal state you have in mind for the world, no matter how carefully you describe it, cannot be the one that others envisage. Language just isn't precise and all-encompassing enough. So we all kept meddling, changing things, changing them back—though not *back* exactly, just to something closer to the way we thought we remembered it.

We kept yanking time about until it broke.

Kempe's close to finishing up—closer than he will ever

realise, because the curtain that will cut him short is the end of his little fragment of world-enough-and-time. And, speaking of time, I have to make my exit right ahead of him, or be obliterated when the tape runs out.

There's another bit of Kempe I found, from another performance. I could catch the end of that show, but it's not the same show and he's not as funny. So instead, I go home.

When I get there, there's some dorky-ass robot bumbling about on the old homestead, much to Miffly's consternation. I'm not in the mood for the Turing test, so I take the thing apart, work out where it came from, rig it up as a bomb and then send it back. Job done. Bish bash bosh.

CHAPTER FOUR

ANOTHER PERFECT DAY at the end of the world.

The same perfect day, you might say. Sufficient unto the day are the events thereof, and this is the day and these are the events. Me and the Soviet Speedster pottering about, master of all I survey. The robots planting and tending and harvesting my fields, and all at once because seasons are *so* last year, you know. And by 'last year' I mean, back when we had years. Remember them? Ah, linear time, so retro!

And so I motor my tractor along the dirt track between the turnips and the olive grove, both promising bumper crops. Miffly lopes along behind with her tongue out, soppy old thing. And when the sun sets, it's the same last sunset, the one the world saves just for me. This is my utopia. This is my reward, for good and faithful service in the Causality

War, and nobody is going to take it from me. They can't. Nothing anyone does can change this perfect final moment of the world. Which is also the first moment of the rest of time, but it's the only moment that matters. By setting up shop here where the regular passage of time recommences, and denying access to the future to all comers, I am saving the unseen future from interference. I am time's gatekeeper, and without me the future would become the same ruin as the past.

Picture history as a tower of bricks, as a child might build. Each block is absolutely dependant on the one below in order to maintain its current position. That's causality (if, at any rate, you're picturing infinite bricks). The key thing is, in that model, it is very important what order the bricks go in. *This* brick is only a blue square because of the shape and colour of the brick below; *that* block is only red because, in the brick it sits on, someone shot a Tsar or two.

And we'd been pulling bricks out and shoving new bricks in, one after the other, and the tower had teetered and tottered but not fallen over, and we told ourselves that was because silly little time warriors like *us* couldn't possibly have an effect on something as big as causality.

It's a lot like when we screwed the climate, to be honest. You never think you're going to affect something as big as that. I mean, I'm just burning a little coal here, right? The planet's very big, this piece of coal or cup of oil or forest of trees, it can't be important in the grand scheme of things. A weird blind spot for a species all too happy to consider itself the centre of the universe in every other way. And look, history was a tough old bird. We kept going back and changing things, intentionally or accidentally. We ran all over her and fought our war, murdering each others' grandparents, applying last-minute CPR to the Archduke of Austro-Hungary, accidentally trekking invasive species into the wrong millennium so that Wordsworth wrote *A host of crawling trilobites* instead of that daffodil nonsense. We pushed causality to breaking point—meaning the universe's basic ability to have one thing sensibly follow another.

And we broke it.

We made too many changes—think of that tower, only none of the bricks are quite in place, all sticking out one side or another. And we're using ever less subtlety as we whip them out and shove them back in. Until someone goes at it with all their might and they push the tower over. It's a good metaphor, actually. Imagine that insanely tall stack of blocks just cascading across a polished nursery floor of infinite dimensions, the whole of history scattering into bits, everything out of order.

And if I stood in that crowd and shot Will Kempe dead—everyone's a critic when it's stand-up comedy night, after all—then I could go to another piece of time and catch one of his later shows, because the chain of causality is well and truly broken. You can't change history any more, not past the jagged trailing edge of any given piece. I call it the Causality War because causality was its biggest casualty. We were the time warriors, and we killed time.

Time was busy for a while after that. And you'll understand that I mean both 'after' and 'a while' based on my personal experience of events, because otherwise things can get tricky when you're trying to spin a narrative. It wasn't just the time warriors, but whole populations of time refugees shuffling from shard to shard, trying to find somewhere to settle down. You'd go to Ancient Athens or the court of Kublai Khan or Cahokia, and there would be embarrassed-looking groups of people wearing the wrong clothes and utterly failing to fit in. It was like the world's saddest renaissance faire played out across the whole of history. And you'd find people wrecking the place, in my experience, either because they were trying to take over some shard, or just incidentally through being there. And still fighting the war.

Nobody remembered what the war was about, but we all remembered that there was a war, and anyone you met who wasn't a time-native was de facto on the other side. And it was by observing that—seeing two groups obliterate Byzantium with high-tech weapons, seeing time agents igniting proxy wars between Medici heirs, salting the earth in the Permian to stop anyone else finding refuge there… It was seeing how everyone was still carrying on that made up my mind as to what I myself would have to do.

I'd already come to the conclusion that 'us' and 'them' weren't meaningful distinctions any more, like I said (and, again, 'already' and 'any more' are my personal anchors and your own time travel mileage may vary) because all those time agent shenanigans meant the original combatants, allegiances and *causes célèbres* had been obliterated, written and rewritten until there was nothing but a hopelessly illegible inkblot. And even if I met a fellow agent who seemed to jibe with me, no guarantee they'd be the same when I rendezvoused with them later and/or earlier (let me tell you, it's frankly embarrassing to clap your fellow time warrior on the shoulder only to find that, from their perspective, it's before the pair of you ever met, and then they're trying to stick a gun up your nose and… take it from me, it's a real faux pas; the social anxiety alone was enough to justify burning it all down).

But really, it was just that, once I'd taken a step back from the whole sabre-rattling jingoism of the war, I could see it wasn't going away and it wasn't getting any better. You'd think people would quietly dismantle all that nonsense after the actual nations and parties and religions they were so keen about no longer existed, or had been unrecognisably mutated by altered chains of events, or were just lying about in pieces on the floor. I mean, if you were so very devoted to some rose-tinted golden age, and you had a time machine, why not just go and live in it and stop trying to convert the rest of poor, broken history to fit? And the answer to that—yes, you at the back, speak up boy!—is that, travel as you might through the vasty deeps of time, you never do find that golden age, that promised land. And it's easier for you to claim that *they* got there first with their wicked time machines and erased the moment when everything was *good* and *right* and *proper*, rather than admit that there never was that much gold in all human history.

A bunch of people with time machines were still fighting the war, and a bunch of other people were just… cluttering up history, panhandling for dollars in every spare epoch, setting up camps on the doorsteps of time, splitting into factions, schisming into warring clans, waving the flags of states that didn't exist yet, or any more, or ever would. And I sat back, having discovered in myself that I was really done with the whole grim business, and saw it all sparking off again, in every jagged-edged piece of history, over and over and forever and the universe never having a moment's peace.

Only I could end the Causality War. I couldn't save history, but perhaps I could save *something*. One perfect moment. Peace in our end times.

And so I hunted them down, all of them.

I mean, that makes me sound considerably more badass than in fact I was. Remember they were all fighting amongst themselves, and most of the time it was just a matter of manoeuvring them so that they discovered each other, *this* agent ending up at the precise Ottoman coffee shop *that* agent frequents. *That* marauding band of revisionists stumbling onto *this* camp of temporal refugees. By the end, there were only a few of them left, hunting each other through the Leningrad ruins or the Warsaw ghetto or the incendiary jungles of the Carboniferous—and you can't even imagine what happens when you bring napalm to somewhere with that level of atmospheric oxygen! In the end, I took up my sniper rifle and my particle sword, my griefing knife and my large piece of wood with a nail in it, and I finished the last exhausted survivors off. I won the Causality War on the very sound technicality that I was the only one left standing at the end of it. I then declared peace and went on to a well-deserved retirement here at the end of all things. There's only one onerous task left, really, and that's to ensure that nobody is ever in a position to set it all off again.

And they do try. There's always someone, some budding genius in one shard of time or other, who finds a way out. They build a time machine from circuits and steel, from brass and glass, from sticks and stones or the flight of birds or pure mathematics, and they travel. And, sooner or later, they come here. Because here's where you go, when you travel forwards in time to see how far you can go. You come to the last day, this last perfect day before the rest of time happens. And I will be waiting.

I have a few quiet weeks on the farm after that. I mean, there's the eighteenth-century French natural philosopher who cogito ergo chrononautums his way into my kitchen and drinks quite a lot of my wine while I build the guillotine outside. And there's the Neanderthal who turns up looking rather confused after banging the rocks together *really* hard one day. But other than that, it's business as usual. I run the farm. I go partying with Jackie Onassis, Lord Byron and Nero. I pick up an even older model of tractor from 1930s Ukraine and spend a few days cleaning off the rust.

I don't fight in the Causality War, and every day you don't fight in the Causality War is a good day, and every good day is the same perfect day, and that's basically my eternal win condition.

Then the alarm goes off again and I get into the Speedster and putter off to see who's come calling this time. Privately

I'm hoping that it'll be something discrete and easily removed from the timeline. Because that last one took a lot of remedial work and now there aren't and never were any Neanderthals, which feels like a bit of an overreaction. But it's like painting, and sometimes you keep trying to get something perfect and it ends up a great big smeary mess. No going back. Which, honestly, should have been the motto for the whole Causality War.

When I get in sight of their time machine, I have a bit of a nasty turn. It's a layered globe model that looks to share a fair amount of technological DNA with mine. Which means it comes from a time and place not unlike my own, with the usual caveat that the time and place I come from don't actually exist anymore and never did. For a moment I'm braced for the shot, for the blade, for the unknown piece of advanced military hardware that's going to end my prolonged and comfortable life here. Did I miss a time warrior? Am I not the sole survivor of the war?

But then a woman's voice is calling out, "Hallo!" across the fields, and I see her and a male companion just standing there in the open, waving at me. They do not look like time warriors. You get to know the look: desperation stains the soul if you stew in it long enough. You can tell someone who literally has nowhere in all of time and space they call home, orphaned from all of causation, and these two aren't it. They're far too comfortable and cheery. I recognise people with a solid *When* behind them, the products of a logical sequence of consecutive events. Lucky, corn-fed, privileged bastards.

They are a good-looking pair, regular features like beauty pageant contestants or TV anchors, wearing white-and-silver matching outfits. Jumpsuits, with puffy moon boots and gloves, like they've come to give me the wisdom of the ancients. Except I've met the ancients and they were just as dumbass as everyone else, and just piling a bunch of enormous stones on top of one another shouldn't be anyone's idea of an achievement. Sort out your healthcare plan and welfare state first, Pharaoh.

I am, by this time, an old hand at estimating the origin point of time travellers. It's my self-appointed career, after all; you expect to develop some on-the-job skills. These clowns must be from somewhen recent, some rare splinter from during the war, perhaps, where someone finagled events so that the war itself hadn't happened, or maybe some time just before things kicked into high gear. Some lost remnant of a replacement timeline I or one of my peers brought about, when things were actually better for a bit. And somewhere out there that shard of time exists, with these happy, smiling people and their time machines. And I smile happily back at the pair of them, tilting my broad-brimmed hat back over my sun-reddened forehead and chewing at my straw, every bit the welcoming yokel. Time to play host, to enjoy some human company, to brush the dust off the big saucepans. Time to engage these two naifs in conversation so that I can find out precisely where and when they set off on this doomed voyage from.

And then I'll go back to their happy little hand's breadth of time and stamp it into the dirt so that not one of those happy, handsome people ever get to step into the timestream again. And, looking at them, I know it won't just be the case of murdering Professor Braniac Boffo the maverick chrononavigator who's sent his sole two protégés to do the impossible. Something institutional has crapped out this perfect pair onto my wheatfields. I'm going to have to obliterate quite a lot of their sunny little society in order to prevent them further desecrating history's cooling corpse. And that's a shame, but somebody's got to do it.

The man's name is Weldon. The woman's is Smantha. "Samantha?" I clarify, but no, apparently it's 'Smantha.' I've been invaded by chrononautic hipsters. But they're engaging enough. They stare at the fields, and the Speedster, and me, and if their eyes were any wider the balls would fall out of their sockets. So damn enthusiastic! You'd think they'd never seen the end of all things before. And they grin and they're always *touching* or putting their arms about each other's waists, and I honestly wonder if they didn't violate the entire fabric of the continuum just to cop an illicit feel or something. All the way home I listen to their innocent chatter, sat in the trailer of the Soviet Speedster. And then we run into Miffly, who's jumped the fence again, bad girl. I hadn't intended them to meet Miffly just yet. In fact, meeting Miffly is generally the last stop in the whirlwind tour of the future I have planned for people. I wait to see just how they take to a ravening allosaur loping alongside the tractor eyeing up its dinner.

They're cool with her, basically. They make all the right noises and tell each other how cute she is—and she *is*, once you get past the teeth and the claws and the terrible breath. By the time I reach the farmhouse, they're scratching her under the chin just where she likes and have made a friend forever. Or at least until I kill them, after which Miffly will likely sulk a bit and then forget, because there's a limit to how much sentiment a large therapod can really hang on to. But they get on well with my pet, and I find myself warming to them. I am, I decide, going to have a fine old evening playing host. I'll get out the *good* wine, dusty bottles rescued from the collapse of time, from governments and from badly-designed cellars. I'll cook. I don't all-out cook often, but the fit has taken me. I am going to push the boat out. And while I'm in the kitchen and they're enjoying a little mammoth-cheese aperitif at the table, we can chat about just exactly where they came from and where the time machines are parked back at their end.

WHEN YOU'RE LIVING on your own, you forget how much fun it is to cook for company. I almost forget what I'm doing after I've got the wine flowing and the nibbles out and I'm melting butter in the big skillet. I talk them through the details of each dish and ingredient, and they eat up the details greedily. I make my standard joke about everything coming from a sustainable source, that's really just for my personal amusement—after all, there's no such thing anymore, not now we broke time. But they get it and they laugh, and I'm really starting to enjoy this hosting lark.

But business comes first.

"You must have come quite a way," I start, as if their time machine had just broken down outside and they came in to use the phone. "Nice place, where you come from, is it?"

They agree that it is, it really is. Quite the perfect place to live. And I look at their white-and-silver clothes and their faces that are devoid of cancer marks and disease scars and any suggestion of childhood privation, and almost ask why they ever left. Because it's horrible out there, in history. It always was, even before we shattered it to bits. It's full of war and plague, starvation, intolerance and misery. But, but, but, I hear you say. But hope, but progress, but the glory of human achievement.

A candle, I tell you. And the rest of it is the hurricane. I have sat in the palaces of the Minoans before the Bronze Age Collapse. I have dined with the egalitarian philosophers of Harappa in the Indus Valley before the world turned and ground them to dust. I have taught whist to Archimedes shortly before a Roman soldier gutted him. And yes, human achievement is a grand and splendid little candle in the great vast night of causality, but there's only so often you can watch it be snuffed out before it's easier to become the snuffer. And so I listen to the two of them fondly tell me how bloody wonderful it is where they come from, and I brown the vegetables. And I poison the dessert wine, because frankly puddings aren't my strong suit when it comes to haut cuisine and it'll save everyone a lot of embarrassment if I can murder these two wunderkinden before they find out how lousy my baked Alaska is.

And there's something about their manner that's starting to

get on my nerves, which will make the whole murdering-them-and-then-destroying-all-trace-of-their-culture a bit easier. There's a sort of giggling, nudge-and-wink going on between them as they look at me. A sort of *shall-we-tell-him-no-not-yet* that's frankly juvenile. I really need to get the goods from them and then maybe pour an early glass of the good stuff.

"Maybe I should come visit, if it's all you say it is," I suggest airily, and Weldon and Smantha agree that yes, yes I absolutely should. They'd be only too glad to show me.

I put my finger up to test the wind, naming a couple of likely centuries I reckon they might have come from. It must be some little shard right on the edge of the desert of dead time that's ground zero for the war. The epoch we were fighting *for*, which every past battle was intended to change. The time of my life, the time I can't go back to. Older history gets shredded into progressively larger chunks, so I can get a fortnight in Elizabeth's London, a sybaritic summer sleeping on Nero's couch or a solid couple of hundred years running away from dinosaurs. But, as you approach the war, the pieces get smaller, and during the war itself, to visit any one moment would be… just that. Each moment, each instant of the decades that made up my life is a separate grain of sand on that lifeless beach. And beyond it… here, the end times, my domain.

So Weldon and Smantha have come from somewhere pretty remarkable, I reckon. Some unusually longitudinous shard of time hard up against the war. Amazed I never came across it, but it's absolutely the sort of thing I have to remove from causality with extreme prejudice. They are some version of the people who turn into the people who start the war, and they already have the weapons to fight it. So, I'm sorry, kids, but I can't allow you to *be*. Nothing personal, but I'm going to go shoot a few grandfathers, and yours'll be among them.

And so I coax and wheedle and feed them some seriously good homemade chow, and they cast each other little sidelong glances full of mischief, like it's *them* playing a trick on *me* somehow. Like I'm not going to dole out some death-by-dessert, the last course of their last supper. But I grin and smile and raconteur until I'm clearing the plates away and wondering if I'll just have to kill them before pudding and reverse-engineer the truth from their transport.

Then I turn round and they're both grinning at me, absolutely delighted with themselves, and Smantha says, "We've got a bit of a confession."

I nod, and if my expression is a bit exasperated then my comedy apron and chef's hat takes away from it.

"We're probably not supposed to tell you," Weldon adds.

"But it's just so, *so* wonderful to meet you," she finishes for him. They're holding hands and finishing each other's sentences. I think I'm going to be sick.

"They're not going to believe it, back home," says he.

"Not that we should tell them!" says she, with the clear indication that they won't be able to keep their damn mouths shut and everyone will have heard the whole story within thirty minutes of their return.

And yet, what story? They went to a nice farm up the time stream and met... me?

"I mean," I tell them, "it's very flattering to my skills as a cook, but I can't see how anyone's going to be *that* interested. Not when you've got the whole of time to visit."

"Oh, we'll do time later," Smantha says dismissively. "We just had to meet you first, though. How could we not? We've read so much about you."

I have a very, very ill feeling about things. I couldn't feel iller if I'd drunk the dessert wine myself, frankly.

"But you really have to come and see," Weldon says. "Right now! Everyone'll be so excited."

"Just tell me when," I croak out. "I'll go dust off the time jalopy. Just tell me, back a hundred years, two hundred, five hundred...?" Desperately clutching at chronological straws.

"Oh, no," they say.

"Not back," says Weldon.

"Forwards," chimes in Smantha.

"Grandfather," they finish together.

CHAPTER FIVE

I MEAN...

No.

I mean, absolutely not, under any...

I am nobody's grandfather. Because I live at the end of time, on the far side of all that wreck of fractured history that's all the war left of the past. I live here, on my farm, in an eternal perfect day just where sane causality picks up again, and that's it. I am the full stop to the sentence that is human history. That's the point.

That's...

I took all the technology of the Causality War and I made a thing, here. I was its only inheritor, after all, and I had all the manuals and receipts and warranties (not that the latter were worth anything anymore, admittedly).

Because, being the sole survivor of the war and, by extension, of all of human history, I didn't know entirely what I wanted to do with my life, save for one particularly strongly held resolution.

Never again.

That thing we did, that broke everything in the universe; which left all of history in a scatter of sharp-edged shards so that nothing led to anything—that war, that lunacy, that terrible, terrible time-to-end-all-times—must never come again. And to that end, I would set a trap. I would create a bottleneck here at the near end of the rest of time. I would ensure that anyone travelling into the future from that broken desert of glass would find only one thing: me. They would find me, and my alarms would go off, and I would find them. And then they would die, and I would go back and ensure that nobody else would ever venture onto the seas of time to wash up on my shore.

And beyond my postepochalyptic ranch, time could just stretch on forever, never to be troubled by any human presence. Never to be broken, maimed, mauled, mutilated or spindled. I was the great gatekeeper, and my watchword was *You Shall Not Pass.*

I have eliminated one hundred and eighty-nine wildly different time travellers who have tried to get into the pristine future to ruin it all. Nobody got past me. There is no white-and-silver art deco utopia to produce a Weldon or a Smantha. There is *no future.* They cannot have come from it.

And yet they sit here in my kitchen, eating my food and telling me I should come visit. And I have lived a life that's all about the grandfather paradox, and now I discover it was the wrong grandfather I was worrying about all the time. I am my own paradox.

I want to murder them and bury them in an unmarked grave and pretend this never happened, but I can't give in to sentiment. I have to know

"I suppose," I tell them, "you'd better show me."

AND IT'S LOVELY. Of course it's lovely. It's as bright and gleaming a future as you could possibly want, the bastards.

I hop in my wartime special and punch in the impossible coordinates. A tomorrow that shouldn't be—which I suppose makes a difference to my usual fare of a yesterday that's about to be edited out of existence, but I would far prefer to stick with what I know.

We materialise in the grandest and most chrome-trimmed parking lot you can imagine, with a big old dome roof and a viewing gallery and at least a dozen of their fancy time machines. Which apparently are upgrades from my own model, because they're from the *future* all of a sudden, and therefore better than me.

I have worked so hard.

I have sweated and strained and *slaved* for there not to be a future, and now I stand next to my poor last-year's-model and look at their wondrous abundance of time machines, and all I can think is, *It's all going to happen again.*

And Weldon and Smantha are beaming and gurning and so happy with their news that they could burst. I wish they *would* burst. I wish the pair of them would swell up like septic limbs and then pop in a great big shower of infected pus. But no, there they are being pleasant and keen and beautiful, and they tell me what a privilege it is to have me as their guest, and how I can have anything I like, and just wait till everyone finds out who's coming to dinner.

I mean.

I mean I just *made* them dinner, and already they're...

I mean, talk about poor guest etiquette. It's *rude*, is what it is. I put a lot of love into that meal. Or if not *love*, then at least murderous guile, but it was still effort and now they're telling me they already had plans for the evening.

Anyway, they dash off hand-in-revoltingly-twee-hand to tell all their friends, and I lean back against my poor battered old time-mobile and try to look as surly as humanly possible, because I don't want to give them the satisfaction. And soon enough, people start to filter onto the balcony above to gawp down at me. Young, beautiful people. Older people who are still achingly beautiful. Children who look like they've been got up in their smartest white-and-silver clothes, hair brushed and faces scrubbed, except they probably look like that every moment of their perfect lives. And they all look a bit like each other, because apparently the utopian future is a bit uncomfortably eugenic. (Which is one more thing the war was probably about, or one iteration of it. What were we fighting the war for? Like Brando in *The Wild One*, 'Whadda ya got?')

And they stare, and I feel like I'm in a zoo, and when I glower up at them they try to pretend they weren't staring, without actually stopping staring, and they're fooling nobody, but I can't exactly stand there and shout at them because that would be rude, and so we've got this stupid social impasse. And I'm still getting stared at.

And then Weldon and Smantha are back with a whole delegation of beautiful, smiling, wildly enthusiastic people, and they're all shaking my hand and gabbling about what an honour it is to finally… I get kissed on the cheek and clapped on the shoulder and hugged, and this guy's crying with joy and that woman is squealing with excitement, and the whole joyous mob of them bustle me through to the next chamber.

There's a party going on. Maybe two hundred people in the immediate environs, and every one of them looking absolutely the picture of health and happiness. Their clothes are gold and silver and white and ultraviolet and zany ziggy zaggy patterns, and some of them have glowing tattoos or gems in their foreheads or bejewelled piercings. Each one is more perfect than the last, and there's music that annoyingly manages to be lively yet also timelessly elegant, and every one of them is having a good time. And they turn to me when I shamble in, yesterday's man straight off the farm with allosaur dung on his boots, and they are just so goddamn *pleased to see me.*

And projected in the air overhead in letters so bright it hurts to look at them is the legend *Happy Founder's Day* with too many exclamation marks.

"What the hell's Founder's Day?" I demand of Weldon and Smantha.

"We just invented it!" they tell me enthusiastically, like they do everything enthusiastically. "Because you're here!"

I get the whirlwind tour after that. They skim me out into the country with their skimmer and I see all those perfect farms laid out one after another, zero carbon footprint, one hundred per cent recycled, environmentally compliant. They show me the forests they planted, the ecosystems they've engineered. They show me the city of domes and towers and flying cars they live in. There are only about a thousand of them, right now, I understand, but even back in the war I remember various groups researching genetic variation tech because they planned to be the only people left when the dust settled. Population size isn't the problem it used to be. Of course, my own postwar plan involved a population of one eking out a hermit's existence in the forever of the end-times, without any posterity at all, so it wasn't anything I had to worry about.

By then, I grudgingly admit that I have worked up an appetite, so it's time for me to enjoy someone else's cooking.

The food is, needless to say, perfect. A succession of tiny dishes, each more delicate in flavour than the last, each complimenting its predecessor and whetting the appetite anew for its successor. Like one of those restaurants where you only really go for the delicious starters, only it's *all* starters and never the belly-bloating stodge of the main course. I am almost weeping by the end. I've never had anything so good. I could eat it forever, and no doubt the food's so healthy that I'm practically getting a full-body workout just from chewing it.

Weldon and Smantha sit to one side of me, and there's a succession of others: older, younger, men, women. They all hold hands and they all smile at me and each other, and the conversation is carefree and witty. People get up and recite impromptu poetry, and somehow even *that* isn't as tedious and awkward as it would normally be.

And we get to that point in the evening where most hosts, be they ever so gracious, would be making is-that-the-time-you-must-be-wanting-to-get-away noises, and I end up on another balcony with Weldon and Smantha and a few others, looking down into the crystal waters of a pool where a bunch of dolphins are performing some kind of dramatic presentation of their own invention. It is very moving. I am very moved. So, so moving. And Weldon and Smantha are whispering to one another in that conspiratorial way they have, that is too innocently charming to be properly annoying. "Shall we show him?" "Yes, oh, we must! What fun!" Like I'm the deaf old uncle everyone loves to patronise. And so they take me to some equivalent of the town square and show me the statues.

Actual statues.

Stat*ues*, plural. Dual, in fact, because there are only two.

They are shown waving—his right hand, her left—and holding hands with each other, and I take this as extreme artistic licence because *he* is very clearly me.

I'm depicted wearing something a bit like what they wear, and I look considerably happier than I ever have at any given moment of my real life. Actually, I look happier there than I have in all the moments of my life added together and multiplied by three. And so does she, the other one, the woman.

She kind of looks like them. Like all of them. And all of them kind of look like me. And that's because when Weldon and Smantha called me grandfather it wasn't exactly hyperbole. I mean, not actual grandfather, not just two generations, but it's me. I am their progenitor. I'm going to meet a nice girl and settle down and have a utopia.

I look at that face. It's a good likeness. The sculptor, or the robot the sculptor programmed, or however it worked, had access to an image of me, and in that image I was waving and smiling and I got the girl and wasn't living under the shadow of the Causality War. I had changed my mind, found hope for the future, and then actually built a future. And now I've seen the future I built, and it's come on really well. It's just fabulous, and everyone's beautiful and happy and perfect and so's everything else. I mean, I know the point of a utopia is that it's the best of all possible places, but this was the best utopia. If there was a utopia contest I'd put money down on it winning.

And I built that. Apparently.

"How does it feel?" Smantha asks me, and I confess I'm a bit overwhelmed.

"I need to get back to the farm, really," I manage, and they look disappointed, and I'm very quick to assure them they've not in any way failed as hosts but it's all been a bit much. And, let's face it, I do actually *have* to get back to the farm and carry on, or else this whole utopia thing is putting the cart before the horse. They are the result of my settling down with a nice girl, and it all goes a bit tits up if I just stay here playing the grand old man.

And they understand that. Of course they do. They are, after all, perfect people from a perfect world where footling social awkwardness has been hunted to extinction.

I wave them off before I step into my time machine, trying to work out how much older I looked, as a statue, compared to the face I see while shaving. How long before I get swept off my feet?

I go back home and look out over the farm. Nothing's changed, but it all seems different. There's a future hanging over it that wasn't there before. Miffly comes bounding over and I scratch her under the chin absently.

That was an adventure, I tell myself.

What food, what company, what music! So perfect, such utopia, wow.

I look out at the sunset, my faithful therapod at my side, and I make the only appropriate resolution.

I am not doing it.

I am not having any of it.

I will not become that smiling chump, and there will be nobody to make a statue of me. Oh, it's all utopias today, but tomorrow it'll be the Second Causality War, and I am not being responsible for bringing that about.

And they were just *too* happy. They were just too perfect. They were too goddamn *twee*.

I am going to make sure they're never even born, the jolly happy bastards. I'd say they will rue the day they ever showed up here, but that won't even be an issue. Because unlike those troublesome venturers from the shattered past, I don't even have to *do* anything to make sure Weldon and Smantha and their friends aren't even born. I just need to make sure that I, their great-great-and-however-many-greats-grandfather, don't hook up with whoever the hell *that* was and, boom, problem solved. It's the grandfather paradox in reverse, in fact, where I just swear never to have kids once someone shows me the future family photo. All I have to do is just carry on as I have been, and they never happen. Every day I just get on with my solitary existence I'm murdering their entire civilization.

And that feels good, in a way that all that glitzy partying and smiling didn't. That, frankly, is a utopia I can get behind.

CHAPTER SIX

I AM SUFFICIENTLY heartened by this revelation that I decide I'm due a proper holiday. It's not often one finds one can save the world by sheer indolence. Usually, when I take a break from the farm to go enjoy myself, there's this scratchy layer of guilt that the work isn't getting done. I don't mean the farm work, because the robots basically have that covered. I mean the real work, the stopping-another-Causality-War work of pouncing on errant time travellers as and when they finally end up in the end times. Except now I'm stopping the war specifically by kicking back and relaxing. I am doing my sworn and solemn duty just catching some rays by the pool.

So, itinerary for a traditional getaway:

First, you've got to travel somewhere. Even I, possessed

of the technological means to go anywhere instantaneously, feel that it's not a proper holiday without some serious time spent crossing the miles getting from A to B, preferably with some utterly unavoidable waiting around.

You need to see some sights, some serious monuments.

A good meal somewhere, too. You'll have noted by now that I am something of both a gourmet and a gourmand.

A night out on the tiles, razzling it up with some party animals.

And a bit of solitude, somewhere you can relax and read a good book.

Of course, I'm going to cheat a bit. I'm not going to try and find a single perfect destination. Time and space is my smorgasbord, after all.

I kick off my spring break by falling in with Odysseus just as he's about to leave the smoking ruins of Troy. I mean, if you're looking for a pointlessly complicated journey with lots of waiting around, you honestly can't beat an angry Greek man spending far too long trying to get across one of the smallest seas in the world. And obviously it's not really *that* Odysseus, because Homer wasn't exactly into biographical accuracy, but he's still a fun guy and so, let's go on a cruise, why not? Oddy and the gang are decent company, the amphoras are overflowing with admittedly watered wine, and they know some impressively filthy drinking songs about nereids.

And, yes, I do change things a bit, and if this shard gets as far as Homer picking up the story for his greatest hits then you might be surprised at some of the new verses. The bit where Odysseus and his crew get into a furious argument at a taverna over how to split the bill should prompt some particularly nuanced use of simile.

After that I do a whirlwind tour of the Sphinxes.

There's one definite advantage to time being shattered irrevocably into a thousand million pieces. Given how long the edifice lasts, you can have as many Sphinxes in as many old Gizas as you like, and it's proved a remarkably tempting prospect to a great many historically significant vandals in various iterations of this timeline or that. So I go see the original, where it's just a big old person-head on the big old lion-body, although admittedly a rather wonky and boss-eyed one so I can see why nobody complained much when they changed it. And then there's a whole host of Pharaohs who got their own face on it, although given the limitations of their sculptural stylisation they all kind of look the same: arched eyebrows, lean cheeks, tubular beards—even the women. There's that one shard where Napoleon went on an epic bender and ordered it reshaped into his image. There's another where it's one of the grandchildren of Genghis Khan because a bunch of agents from one time faction or another thought that a successful Mongol conquest of Europe and North Africa would achieve... well, I forget what it was we or they were trying to achieve. I forget if it was even we or they. Seemed like a good idea at the time, is as far as my memory supplies. And the problem with time travel, and what we considered to be the infinite resilience of the continuum, was that you get used to just acting on whatever seems like a good idea at the time, until you break time and there aren't enough good ideas in the world to put it back together again. Humpty Dumpty eat your heart out.

And yes, there's a Sphinx out there with my face. I am not proud. It was an infantile thing, to spend eight years pretending to be Osiris by way of high-tech trickery in order to get them to build it that way. I have regrets. I don't go and see that one.

I'm peckish by then, so I review the restaurants within easy reach, which means all of them that still exist in some shard or other, across the whole of human history.

I go for starters with Caligula, not because I like Caligula, but because when a petulant and homicidal man-god demands the best deep-fried dormice in the Empire, he damn well gets them. Also, I get to sit next to Claudius, who tends to keep his mouth shut and not tread on the punchlines of my jokes. For a main course I fancy some really good rare steak. In my day, which is now irreparably lost since the entire run up to and duration of the Causality War got completely obliterated by that war's end, we were all vegetarian. By then it was a necessity, to save the planet. I honestly think someone invented the time machine just so they could go grab a burger from the 1980s when the urge took them. Anyway, turns out saving the planet by eating soy was a bit of a non-starter given how we destroyed the entirety of history, but it was a good idea at the time. At any rate, I do feel I can go get a really good steak without feeling guilty about it.

I end up in the Palaeolithic. It's not exactly a restaurant, per se. More a camp fire. And mein host is, admittedly, called something like Og and he only takes barter, so I have to scare up a sled-full of hides before I arrive. Still, the steak... You haven't lived until you've had a good bloody haunch of mammoth. The whole process of being scared off a cliff onto sharp rocks gives it a real gamey flavour you don't get anywhere else. And it doesn't matter that Og isn't much of a conversationalist, what with language not really being a thing yet, because everyone's too busy chewing.

And for dessert I end up in a TGI Fridays in Reading town centre in the mid-1990s because they do an ice cream cocktail that I'm particularly partial to, and I defy you to judge me.

On to the party, and for that it's Paris in 1832, when the revolutionaries are manning the barricades in perhaps the most doomed of all the Parisian uprisings, more so even than the poor bloody Commune. A pack of students and lefties and idealists with muskets who know the rest of the city hasn't risen to join them, but are bloody well not backing down even though the army pitched up that afternoon. And that night, before the end, they throw a truly epic party, the student rave to end all student raves. They drink, they make love, they swear everlasting loyalty to each other. When I was there the first time, I was sad, seeing all that youth about to pour itself in blood all over the ground. Now, I can be philosophical. Everyone dies, after all; every good time ends. Time *itself* ended. They are doomed, but in their doomed moment they live forever, and at least they had a good time for one night. Sometimes that's all that counts. And this time round I teach them the rousing songs from the relevant musical and we bellow it out at the army camped out there, and at the uncaring populace of Paris. And they actually do Hear The People Sing and next morning the entire city's up in arms and I've screwed over history again. And it doesn't matter. Because this is just one bit of it, and it changes nothing else. I still feel good about it, though.

I'm whistling the tunes across the next two hundred million years, because after that it's a bit of a wind-down in Permian Park.

This is a long shard of pre-ecological collapse, somewhere coastal. I take a good book. There's a shard I know where Agatha Christie's just settling down to write a new one, and it's my habit to pitch up like the man from Porlock and talk inanely at her just before she does, meaning the book she ends up turning out is different each time and so I have an infinite supply of enjoyably trashy murder mysteries. And sometimes I push the envelope a bit with the conversational topics of my Porlockery, which is why this particular country house drama involves an Indian Army colonel with a giant battle-mech (although it does turn out to be just a red herring).

All good things must come to an end, though, and eventually I've finished my book, lying out in that high-quality sunshine you only get when the Earth's about to fry in a poisonous paroxysm of climate change. Time to get back to the ranch. Miffly will be getting anxious and will probably have eaten most of the sheep by now. (Shopping list item: go rustle some more sheep on the way home.)

And so I trudge back to the time machine and set it as

far forward as it goes, or at least as far forward as it used to go, before Weldon and Smantha showed me there was actually a further forward. *But not for long,* and I chuckle indulgently to myself, even though the precise wording doesn't really make any sense in context. What I *can't* do, really, is go back to the future of my future and see if they're still there, because that all gets a bit Schrödinger's Cat, and the act of going looking for them might perpetuate their existence or something. I mean, I'm just a multidimensional time warrior, don't ask me to explain the math.

When I get back, someone's fed Miffly.

That's the most obvious thing. I just stand there, staring at the trough, which is full of chewed-over *Parasaurolophus* bones. And she's only supposed to have the stegosaur, but, like any pampered pet, she vastly prefers to eat dinosaurs that won't even evolve for tens of millions of years after her species becomes extinct. And someone knows that, and has been indulging her.

And the door of the farmhouse is off the latch. And given the latch is a very high-tech piece of chicanery indeed, that's also worrying.

Someone's been through my things. They've been relatively subtle about it, but I've fallen into a lot of fussy habits over the indeterminate time I've lived here, and I can see my papers have been moved. I can see my diary has been read. Which will have been a real disappointment, because there's only one entry and it reads, *Today I have decided to start a diary.*

I am frozen, right there in the house. I panic. What's gone

wrong? I set the alarms and everything; if any time traveller from anywhere whatsoever turned up on my patch, I would have cancelled the holiday and hotfooted it over straight away. I would have arrived in the nick of time to sort them out, because that's how time travel works. And there was nothing. Nobody has tripped the wires. The integrity of the space-time continuum remains unviolated.

And yet someone's been here.

Someone's *still* here, maybe.

Either that or someone's circumvented my alarms and can just come and go as they please, and I'd prefer not to believe that because it would invalidate my entire self-made existence here. I am the warden, the gatekeeper, the guardian of history. Nobody gets by me.

I tool up with all the detection technology I can lay my hands on and go out hunting, roaming the range with Miffly pacing alongside the Soviet Speedster, looking for… anything, really. And it's Miffly who does the finding, in the end, because allosaurs have a really good sense of smell, and because I forgot to put batteries in most of the detectors. Miffly finds the campsite first—just the cold ashes of a fire, but *someone* was bivouacked out in the fields, where they had a view of the farmhouse. Cautious, apparently; didn't know I was out on vacation. And then Miffly finds the time machine.

I know the model. I mean, not to puff myself up too much, but I am history's premier expert on the subject. There's no spotter's guide needed for this one, though. It's the same type as Weldon and Smantha used when they came visiting.

For a moment I just assume that's it. I've been out-teched, and they can evade all my alarms. Then I take a good look at the machine and it's honestly not much of an improvement on my own wartime model. I guess blissful utopias don't give you much of an incentive to fix what isn't broken. And if there's one damn thing my alarms are good for, it's picking up war-epoch arrivals. That was, after all, my primary concern when I was setting up here. So, what...?

There is, I realise, only one logical possibility.

They came back at the same instant I did. They were there in that never-to-be utopia that I'm trying so indolently to make un-happen. When I got into my wartime special, they hopped into this next-year's-model. We came back simultaneously. It's the only way it could have worked without tripping the alarms.

When I was planning my itinerary, they were watching the house. Perhaps they were clutching an autograph book, desperate for the Founder to do them some words of encouragement and a humorous doodle.

It's already started. This is why I have to ensure they never happen. Even when I hunt down and kill my new fan, it causes a chain of contradictions. History, meaning the actual continuous chain of causality stretching forwards from my end-times ranch into the future, gets put under strain. And, left to their own devices, those utopian bastards would eventually take one trip too many, have one too many time-travelling descendants, start a new war, invent a fresh batch of Causality Bombs, shatter the future just like we shattered the past.

Did I mention the Causality Bombs? For when regular time travel just can't mess up continuity enough.

I need to track down my visitor and dispose of them as efficiently as possible before things get out of hand and my farm becomes a tourist destination for every gawper and sightseer from the future.

There follows a few days of me getting all the surveillance kit out of the attic and trying to remember which bit connects to what and how to rewire six centuries' worth of different models of plug. At the end of it all I have some drones and some cameras and a load of other kit to try and spot the intruder, who is remaining surprisingly coy given the whole cultural obsession with boisterous enthusiasm I marked on my one and only visit to their misbegotten time period. Then I go hunting again, searching my entire domain for any trace of them. Their time machine is still here, after all—now surrounded with tripwires and traps and some angry sabre-tooth tigers for good measure. And if *it's* still here, so is my visitor.

And of course they get into the farmhouse again while I'm out. I get back to find they've been sitting on my chair, eating my porridge, though thankfully not sleeping in my bed.

They disabled almost all the sensors and traps and shenanigans I set up. And then left a load of crumbs and a half-eaten baguette on the kitchen table. From that I know that they know that I know, and are very pointedly letting me know that they know I know they know I know. Or… possibly I'm rabbit-holing too deep, but there's definitely some multi-stranded structure of shared knowing going on between us.

And they've missed a drone. They were so careful to switch off every camera, so that those crumbs were the sole taunting message to me, but I got slipshod when putting one of the drones together, and didn't link it to the network properly. It's been sitting there, taking pictures and not sending them to my central data store, meaning (as it's a cheap, crappy little thing) that it has just the one most recent shot in its memory when I find it. A grainy, rather retro piece of image recording, but good enough for my purposes.

There they are, sitting at my table, helping themselves to the fruits of my labours.

There *she* is.

And I feel a shock of revelation, a yawning pitch of dismay, because I've seen her before.

Not in the flesh, but in the unliving reproduction. It's *her*, the other statue, the Eve to my Adam. My destined soulmate, co-founder of the bloody utopia, has come to meet me.

CHAPTER SEVEN

THIS WILL TEACH me to go gallivanting off on holiday when there's work to do. I should have tracked down a damn nuke and sent it ahead to the utopians gift-wrapped, with a label saying *Don't open till Founder's Day*. Except that would likely still leave enough bits of their time machine fleet to cause me problems later, or indeed before. I need to make them never-have-been instead, and that's going to be difficult when my bride-to-be has tracked me down to my lonely old farm and is lurking about on the grounds.

I am going to have to commit pre-uxoricide. It won't be the worst thing I've done. In fact, when you think about it, most of the people I murder haven't really done anything to me at all, save been incautious in venturing the wrong way across the fourth dimension. When I get hold of the future Mrs Me and feed her to Miffly or run over her with a combine harvester, it will be personal. There will actually be a real and immediate motive. Any court in the land would, if not absolve me of the crime, then at least convict me without needing to take some sort of course in advanced chrono-physics. She's a trespasser and she's come to ruin my life by somehow making me happy enough that I settle down with her and found a gloriously twee society of facile wankers like Weldon and Smantha. And if that's not a good enough reason to seek someone's death, then I don't know what is.

I start off trying to do things the old-fashioned way and have Miffly track her down. I get myself up in proper huntin', shootin' and fishin' clothes—tweed plus-fours and jacket and flat cap—and I get myself a proper huntin' and shootin' shotgun, one with a decent laser sight and homing AI drone bullets, because if you're going to do a thing, do it properly. I swear, these bullets are so smart that if my intention was to hunt grouse then, the moment after I fired them, the shells would go borrow my time machine, track down the closest common ancestor of all grouse and explode it. Which wouldn't actually exterminate grouse because of the woefully disjointed state of time, but they're only bullets, cut them some slack.

And anyway, it's all for nothing because I don't so much as catch sight of her. And Miffly's no damn help. Miffly's been got at, frankly. She might be several tons of ravaging therapod dinosaur, but the old girl is also just a big softy; feed her and rub her tummy and she's yours forever. And my security cameras catch several instances of the future Mrs Me turning up while I'm asleep, dodging all my tripwires and alarms, and making a fuss of Miffly. So much for the savage vigilance of my faithful reptilian hound, unfortunately. So much for the old fashioned way—and if hunting someone down with a dinosaur isn't old fashioned I don't know what is.

I go to the robotics lab and programme a fleet of drones to find her instead. About a hundred of them, from hand-sized to thumbnail-sized, each of them based on tech from a different epoch, a separate shard of time. There are little helicopters and clockwork birds of brass and gems, steel beetle simulacra and even a thing like a floating jellyfish made of plastic bags. I programme them and wind them up and send them all out to go hunting. And I sit at home with a handful of guns and the keys to my fastest tractor, ready to go after my darling wife-to-be with some large calibre ammo the moment my robot servants track her down.

This also fails. The future Mrs Me is being *very* coy. In fact, soon enough I find some of my robots hanging about the farmhouse like lazy employees, watching *me* for *her,* because apparently she's a bit of a wiz with the old robots herself and has reprogrammed them. I make sure I give her a really good view of my best unamused face before shutting them off. I'm of a mind to send them back to the factory with a strongly worded complaint, but I think in most cases those factories—and the societies from which they arose—don't actually exist any more (or have now never existed). Ergo the warranties are probably void.

What I'm getting from this is that the future Mrs Me is a bit nervous of meeting her beloved. I should be hurt, but admittedly I haven't exactly been hiding my homicidal intent, and so a few nerves on her part are perfectly understandable. It's a big moment, when you meet the man who's going to be the love of your life, and having him determined to murder you is only adding to the pressure. I feel a bit sorry for her, to be honest. I mean, I'm not really the Bluebeard type, but I appreciate that first impressions are probably casting me in that light.

Not sorry enough that I'm not going to kill her, though. It's the whole future of the future at stake, after all. No hard feelings, eh?

But I appreciate the poor innocent is a bit tentative about meeting me, and she's not just going to turn up on the doorstep wearing a big white dress and veil and lugging around the Bishop of Bath and Wells with a marriage licence. I need to try a different tack.

So I find myself a nice glade. I've got some good woodland on the estate. I go hunting in it sometimes, and at other times I just wander and enjoy the facsimile of nature that I've induced to grow here, the ecosystems I've transplanted and species I've saved or re-engineered.

I find a nice big grove: bluebells, oaks, squirrels, all very picturesque. I lug a table out there—it's a big table, and I'm being very open about it, and doubtless she sees me doing it. I set it up with a couple of chairs. I go sit there, not even clutching my shotgun. Not even accompanied by a high-tech death robot or pack of slavering dimetrodons. Just me, peaceful as you like.

And she stays away, but I sense I've got her interest. The next day I turn up with a chess set, just in case she's in a gaming frame of mind. After that, I try a last generation console with a couple of VR headsets, because frankly I never really liked chess that much. After that it's a mint-in-box set of *Ticket to Ride*, the rare Hutchinson Games edition from where Europe split into a thousand different states and the board is an insane mass of intertwining branch lines. She doesn't fancy that either.

On the eighth day I turn up with a bottle of the good wine and a couple of goblets that I nicked from Henry VIII and sit there like we're about to play guess-which-is-the-poisoned-one, and perhaps this relatively candid approach is what leads to her emerging from the trees.

She is still wearing the white-and-silvery clothes of the Utopians, which are probably self-cleaning and self-renewing. Her dark hair is cut short. Her face is sharp-chinned—elfin, one might say. If I had a type, then doubtless she'd be exactly my type. As it is, I'm going to kill her so that I can obliterate the entire civilization that produced her, so types don't really come into it. But now I've actually got her here, there's no reason to be rude. I gesture at the other chair and she approaches cautiously, eyes fixed on me.

I give her my best smile, because we're in endgame territory now. Tomorrow, after digging the grave, I can get back to business as usual. Honestly, the last few days since I discovered her presence have been really quite stressful.

"I didn't catch your name, when they showed me the

statues," I say blithely. "I think it was just Mr and Mrs Founder or something."

She sits and takes the goblet when I slide it over, but she doesn't drink—and, given how lethally poisonous the contents are, this shows an annoying level of awareness in her.

I think for one horrible moment she's going to say "Eve," because that utopia of hers really is so very twee, but in fact she's called Zoe, and I can't really find any deep literary resonance in that.

"I understand this must be a bit frightening for you," I say in what even I realise, after the fact, is a colossally patronising tone. "You must have seen those statues every day. And now I'm here in the flesh."

I check her face for adulation, awe and/or romantic inclinations, and don't really find any of the above. Her expression suggests that, in the flesh, I'm not really a match for the sculpture. And admittedly they did idealise my physique a bit, in the memorial, but that's no excuse for being impolite.

Still, "There you are," she says at last. "In the flesh." She toys with her goblet, very careful to not get even a drop of liquid on her skin. She has a pleasant, light voice, but there's a definite edge to it.

"Look," I tell her, feeling the sudden need to at least be honest with her before I kill her, "I appreciate this has probably been quite a shock. I'm not the man they set you up for. I am not husband material. I am not for redemption. I don't have a mad former wife in the attic who will conveniently resolve our narrative differences before shuffling out of the story. I am genuinely mad, bad and dangerous to know, and in at least three versions of events that's something Lord Byron ends up saying about *me*. So I'm genuinely sorry that things aren't working out the way you expected. I'm sure you had all sorts of idealistic dreams about how this day would go, and I appreciate that, what with hunting you across the moors with gun and dinosaur, things haven't turned out as you expected."

"Oh, you think?" she says, and apparently somewhere amongst the gems of that utopia is a fine vein of sardonyx.

You know, like 'sardonic.' Because she was being...

Look, I am a time warrior and occasional murderer first and foremost. I leave the poetry to Byron.

"It's a nice set-up you've got here," she tells me. "You've got it rigged so anyone travelling from the past ends up on your doorstep. Very clever."

"Thank you." It's nice to be appreciated, even by your victims. Maybe especially by your victims.

"And then you kill them."

"I do, yes."

"Huh." She doesn't actually sound that impressed, which is irksome.

"It's more complicated than that. I have to work out where they've travelled from, so I can eliminate their ability to travel. Otherwise I'd be knee-deep in people coming to see where their friends had got to. I'm not running a holiday resort here, you know."

She nods philosophically. "I suppose."

"Look –" And I'm going to kill her, so why I feel the need to justify myself, I don't know. "It's actually quite complicated. I mean, I am basically the only thing standing between the end of all time as we know it." And I realise after I say it that it doesn't actually make grammatical sense, and she *smirks*, which is infuriating. "I was in the war!" I tell her. "You don't know what it's like. You young people with your utopias, never having to work for anything. Some of us had to fight for everything we had. Actually, scratch that, some of us had to fight for everything, everything there ever *was*."

"Sure," she says. "How's that working out for you?"

"Well –" I start, all full of righteous anger, and then have to admit, "Actually everything there ever was kind of ended up completely ruined because of all the fighting we did for it, so not so well, to be frank. But for that very reason I am damn well going to stop it happening *again*, and that means we can't be Mr and Mrs Founder, unfortunately. And I'm sure you're a very nice girl and everything, but I really need to murder you now. Look, can you just drink the wine? It'll be very quick and painless and save me a great deal of bother."

"Oh, well if you put it like *that*..." she says, with more of that sardony.

She looks a bit depressed by all these developments, or at least weary. What with me hunting her, and her sleeping rough, she probably hasn't had a great deal of rest in the last few days. And she'll have grown up dreaming of this meeting with me, the grand union of perfect soulmates. And now she's met me and it's not what she was led to believe and it's the story of arranged marriages the world over. And she can't even go back to her parents and beg them to call it off, because if they call it off then *their* parents (and so on back through the generations) won't get to exist.

So it's understandable if she's a bit miffed by the whole business, but think about how *I* feel.

She's not making any attempt to swig the wine. Maybe I should have done the *one of the cups is poisoned, oh, no, which can it be?* routine, but I'm also feeling a bit frayed and in no mood for showmanship. And last time I tried that trick, I found myself in urgent need of an antidote because I can never remember whether I've switched the goblets or not.

"So…" I say. Because there are awkward social situations and then there's sitting with your intended spouse who is aware you're trying to murder her and, simultaneously, prevent her from ever having been born. And I need to go check on the sheep in the top field, so if she could just…

"So," she says, standing up and kicking the chair back. I blink at her, and then the three hyaenodons come out of the trees behind her, monsters as big as ponies, drooling rabies all over my nice clean glade. They are the most malign animals I ever saw. Their eyes don't actually glow red like the pits of Hades but they might as well, and if I were to look close enough I reckon even their fleas have eyepatches and carry flick-knives.

Zoe takes a step back and the beasts pad to either side of her, their hungry gaze fixed on me.

I run away.

They give chase.

Today is not working out how I expected, so Zoe and I have that much in common anyway.

The killer robots I had waiting to go annihilate *her* meet the prehistoric monsters she got hold of to devour *me* in a kind of cross-time mutually-assured destruction, and I don't slow down until I'm behind the walls of the farmhouse.

Sitting at my kitchen table, I scratch my head. What, precisely, was *that* about? I mean, she's here to perpetuate her society by way of hooking up with me. Now I will freely admit I am not exactly a prize catch when contrasted with the whole run of historical manliness, but right now I'm literally the only game in town. And she very much needs me alive. As such, the prenuptial present of some rabid carnivores is perplexing, to say the least. I feel a great need to quiz her about it, as I sense I've missed out on some nuance of the situation that might prove rather important. But it's also very much the case that my best opportunity to sit down and chat has passed.

After some further hunting not only fails to locate her but also leads to my narrowly avoiding some deadfalls, tripwires and explosive devices she's set for me, I hit upon the idea of leaving radios about the place, just simple two-way things, so that while I hunt her and she tries to dummy me into traps, we can at least have a dialogue. I would like to understand what's going on before I kill her—or, I'm forced to concede, before she kills me.

A few more days of cat and mouse go by, with the role

of cat being passed back and forth. I nearly get her with a remote-control pterodactyl with a bomb strapped to its head. She comes close with a swarm of disassembling nanobots. We keep each other on our respective toes.

Eventually, the radio I carry with me crackles into life. I've endured long enough, and harried her hard enough, that she wants to talk about it.

"Why don't you just die?" is her opening gambit, and I appreciate her frankness. "You must have lived long enough."

"I don't know," I confess. I'm staked out in a hide, sniper rifle in hands, watching a copse of trees that I reckon she's probably lurking in. "I've been back and forth so much, you lose track. I haven't aged in a while. I think I broke my biological clock."

"Boo hoo for you," she says unsympathetically. "You know you can't live forever, right? I mean, back where I come from, you're not around. Just that dumb statue."

"All the more reason for me to get rid of the place," I say philosophically. "Speaking of which, why all the hostility, if you please? I mean, you need me. Correct me if I'm wrong, but me remaining alive has got to be the cornerstone of your game plan, right?"

"I'm correcting you," she tells me. "You're wrong. Also, that's a horrible mixed metaphor." And then the heat-seeking missile crests the horizon and I'm up and running, activating my countermeasures so it ploughs off into the ground half a mile away and ruins my cabbages, damn her. And then I see the stampede of aurochs coming over the hill, because she's been a bit more belt-and-braces this time. So, in short, there's quite a lot of running for the next hour or so, and we don't get to continue the conversation until I'm back at the farmhouse. Miffly's mooching about outside, already fed, so I know Zoe's been about. In fact, I find she's raided the larder and taken the last of the good cheese. And as the timeline that cheese came from has been edited out of existence, that really was the *last*.

"What," I demand of the radio, "did I ever do to you? I mean, except repeatedly try and kill you, but you make it sound like it's *personal*."

"You make it sound like you're such a catch," she tells me.

"That is very hurtful." I sigh. "Let me guess, there's some futuristic hunk back home you had your eye on, and now you're forced to get together with scruffy farmer me."

"No," she says. "There is no 'hunk,' thank you very much. It's just... you make it sound as though I *want* to kickstart that place."

"Well, yes," I agree. "You do. That's what you're here for."

"You think so?"

"I do think so, yes."

"Well, they thought so as well," she agrees. "I mean, they all spotted it from when I was about twelve, that I was the spit of the woman they had the statue of. They'd been wondering where that woman came from, and then there I was, and they knew that all they needed to do was make the introductions and hey, presto, they'd make their creation myth a reality, right?" And while she's speaking

I'm programming my hunter-killer drones to home in on her location.

"All my damn life after that, it was *founder* this and *founder* that, such an honour here, so lucky-lucky there. And nobody ever asked if I wanted any part of it."

"Yes, yes," I say impatiently. "Born in a perfect utopia, everyone fawning on you, chosen one, poor you with your first world problems."

"I don't know if you've ever lived in a utopia," she tells me, "but it is tedious as anything. Everyone is so damn *nice* all the time. Because if you're not nice, you don't belong. You get repurposed."

I prick up my ears. "Oh?"

"They scrub your brain until it's squeaky clean and then you're nice like everyone else. I was the only one they couldn't do it to, because they were worried about interfering with the causality of how they came about. I was the one person who knew that their utopia was rubbish. And the one person they needed to make it happen."

I have her coordinates now. "That's nice. So what happens now?"

"That depends. Have you drunk your tea yet?"

I look at the cup. With all this talk and telemetry, it's gone cold. I decide that making a fresh brew is probably the wise move, rather than bunging this one in the microwave.

The drones are on their way, but I have a feeling she'll be able to bring them down or even send them back. She's a resourceful little monster.

"Look," she says over the radio, "it's nothing personal,

but I'm going to have to kill you. Because I have seen the future, and it's twee. And I hate them and I'm not going to be their fairy godmother, and the only way I can be absolutely sure they won't *be* is with you dead."

I mull that over. In the distance the sound of my drones being detonated prematurely is like a little Fourth of July.

"I can respect that," I tell her.

Things just got interesting.

CHAPTER EIGHT

THERE FOLLOWS A fairly eventful week of attempted homicide. Zoe proves remarkably adept at this, which makes me wonder just what nasty little backrooms her utopia harbours. I send prehistoric monsters and she domesticates them. She re-wires my robot assassins, fouls the targeting of my drones, disarms my traps and avoids stepping on my landmines. When I drop a Buick on her camp from low orbit, she gets out just before the impact. And she doesn't even touch the tempting but lethally poisonous picnic basket I leave out in a tranquil glade for her to find.

And in between trying to exterminate her, I'm having to do quite a bit of dodging myself. There are venomous spiders in my shoes when I get up in the morning and speckled serpents in my bed when I put my head down at night. When I take a tour of the fields, a couple of the agricultural robots do their level best to decapitate me with their threshing attachments. The next day, I feel the Soviet Speedster isn't running quite right and find that's because of a bomb wired to the rev counter. The only thing that saves me is that Zoe's set it to explode once I reach a certain speed which this particular Son of Communism has never really approached. When I stand up after disarming the device, a stray shot from a long-distance rifle puts a hole in my straw hat. Life on the farm is getting really quite bracing.

That night, I take stock. Zoe is out there somewhere, probably engaged in similar strategising. She has, to date, not managed to kill me, but in the minus column of the ledger she remains aggravatingly un-killed in turn. I feel the match between us remains at a solid no-score draw so far, but given that it's only best of one, that doesn't help either of us.

And I've been murdering errant time travellers for quite a while, not to mention my wartime career of state- or faction-sanctioned mass murder before that—and indeed the genocide of entire timelines every time I swatted an insect I wasn't supposed to. Zoe, on the other hand, has turned out to be an extremely gifted amateur who's in serious danger of challenging me for the end-times all-comer murder trophy.

And I am surprised to find that I feel relatively chill about it. Not that I'm exactly cheering her on, but at least the worst that can happen is still better than the way things are going to go if we *don't* murder each other. Which is to say, even if I slip up and she gets me, that *still* means that Smantha and Weldon's precious Utopia doesn't happen. My ultimate sacrifice will actually mean something (technically it will mean the *absence* of something, but that's still more meaning than anything in the war).

Eventually, though, I admit to myself that I need help. I've been the proverbial lone wolf for a long time. I am, after all, the sole survivor of humanity to make it to the end times, the one living veteran of the Causality War. Fixing things with my own hands has been a long-held habit, because when you're constantly rearranging the sequence of events from the Cretaceous on up, you can never be sure that any other pair of helping hands won't spontaneously have never existed.

So, I get my time machine, remove the explosive device Zoe has taped to it, and go on a bit of a recruiting drive.

I am, I may as well admit, not a very good person. I am a bad person, in fact. But I feel that the task of preserving the future of time requires a bad person who won't shrink from doing bad things.

And, if there's one thing that the various bits and pieces of history have in abundance, it's bad people, so I draw up a shopping list and go to scoop up some real stinkers. I am putting together a hit squad of the very worst that time has to offer, and Zoe is going to get the nastiest kind of applied history lesson when I get back with the troops.

It's quite the whirlwind tour of depravity, believe you me, but I reckon one thing I have over Zoe is that I know the shattered map of time better than she does. I know where to go to get my hands dirty. I know, in most cases, *multiple* versions of some bad, bad people and I can pick the very least pleasant iteration of them, the broken finger of causality where they were the worst they could ever be. That said, I am rushing it a bit, because I really, really can't wait to get back to the farm with my posse and see the look on my poor intended's face. So some of my choices are maybe a little suboptimal.

I go and get Edward Teach, or Blackbeard, to you, because he's big and scary, even though he was maybe a bit better at making people scared of him than actually doing scary things—a lot of being a pirate is in psyching out the opposition—and he turns out to be dead drunk on rum when I talk him into the trip, and he never really sobers up after. I schmooze Elizabeth Bathory by promising her a bathtub of Zoe's blood and that time travel can keep her young (which may well be true, who knows?). I offer Ashurbanipal of Assyria conquests beyond the dreams of an Iron Age tyrant. I throw Gilles Garnier, so-called Werewolf of Dole, a bone and offer La Quintrala a map to El Dorado for when she gets back. After this I look over my troops and reckon I'm a bit short of actual muscle, given how sodden Blackbeard is. So I change tack and go grab the meanest Richard Cœur de Leon I can lay my hands on because, despite the glowing report history gives of him, he really is a self-centred arrogant bastard, but at the same time he can swing a dirty great sword with the best of them. Inspired by that idea, I also go find Achilles and offer him a threesome with any two Patrocles he fancies if he can just rid me of my little prenuptial problem. And, yes, Achilles qua Homer isn't exactly historical, but one of my time-war colleagues did their level best to make the Trojan War happen and so I have a few heroic oddballs in my back pocket. After that I go to gay Paris—the city, not the Homeric character—and tell Robespierre about the glitzy Utopia, which all sounds distressingly aristo to him, and so he rounds up a band of sock-hatted revolutionaries and heads into the future with me. And Stalin; I go grab Stalin because who doesn't want Stalin? That done, we all assemble at the farm, and I stand on a box with Miffly beside me and give them their marching orders. We are going hunting, lads and lasses!

By that time, my drones have located her again, and usually that's a bad sign because she tends to reveal herself only when she has something planned. Right now I reckon the something *I* have planned is going to knock the socks off whatever sad menagerie of Pleistocene predators or booby traps she's thrown together, though, and so off we go to meet her. I am very, very keen to see the look on Zoe's face when she sees all the work I've put into this. I want her to be impressed with the sheer lengths of murderous unpleasantness I've gone to for her sake. I mean, you expect a bit of gratitude, when you make this sort of effort.

We draw up, me on the Speedster and my lynch mob riding a variety of horses, motorcycles, giant mutant dogs, robot beetles and whatever else I had in the stable. And there's Zoe.

She isn't alone.

I feel a keen stab of disappointment. I thought I'd been so clever! I thought I'd surprise her. I wanted to see her reaction. "For me?" she'd cry, before being hacked to pieces by my pack of murderers.

Only she's been busy, too. She's obviously got past all the barriers I placed around her time machine, or else nicked one of the others from my warehouse. She's plainly taken the time to get familiar with the shattered expanse of history. She's done exactly what I've done. She's gone to find some help.

I suppose I should be flattered.

I see Gilles de Rais down there, a Bluebeard to counter my Blackbeard. There's the demented sorcerer Peter Niers, and Duke William of Normandy, already eyeing up that crown Richard Lionheart's wearing and fancying the look of it. I see Black Agnes Douglas and half the clan of the cannibal Sawney Beans, and you'd be a brave man to sample the breakfast they've been cooking up for Zoe's troops. She's got Attila the Hun *and* Vlad the Impaler, apparently engaged in a furious argument over the most pointlessly extravagant way to execute your enemy after they've surrendered to you. I count three different Jack the Rippers, plus Ching Shih and a dozen of her eighty thousand pirates. Plus a rather baffled-looking Tomas de Torquemada, because even the Spanish Inquisition didn't expect *this*.

She's got Hitler. She actually went full Godwin and got Hitler. *And* Stalin. A slightly younger Stalin than my Stalin. She got Hitler *and* Stalin.

Our armies of utter bastards face off against each other,

edging closer and closer. As general, I go take my position on a rise to overlook the battle. After a short while Zoe joins me. We maintain a prudent arm's length distance between us, but honestly we're both more focused on what's about to kick off down below than on cutting each other's throats right then.

"Stalin *and* Hitler is cheating," I say.

"I don't see why. *Achilles* is cheating, he never even existed."

"Says the woman with three Jack the Rippers."

"Eh." She shrugs. "You go to get a Jack the Ripper and he turns out to be some effete aristocrat who only really has the guts to butcher helpless women. So you go to a different shard and find another version, and he's even worse and... before you know it you're up to your neck in Rippers and they're all a bit crap, really."

The fight's begun, by then. It is...

Strangely hilarious. Because none of them really know how to fight each other. Most of them are actually not as terrifying as their reputation, or else they earned that reputation by dint of armies they don't currently have access to. Gilles de Rais and Edward Teach are just tugging on each other's beards and roaring. The Stalins get into a knock-down drag-out wrestling match. Robespierre turns out to faint at the sight of blood when it isn't blue. Torquemada gets eaten by the Beans, and he was nominally on *their* side. And that's a further flaw with our skirmish, because neither of us really did the requisite team-building exercises, and so most of our murderers forget just who's with them and who's the enemy. The entire thing breaks down into an every-murderer-for-themselves skirmish in a muddy field.

Oh, there are some highlights. Ching Shih takes on Achilles blade-to-blade and kicks his ahistorical arse. William impales Richard's heart at the same time as Richard cuts off William's conk. Zoe and I applaud politely, like we're at the cricket. We point out particularly deft flourishes to each other. Elizabeth Bathory stabs up Vlad the Impaler, possibly because her idiot husband styled himself on the man and she's been wanting to do that for ages. The Rippers get into a fight with each other over which of them is the Rippest. Ashurbanipal, without an Empire to back him up, gets his Assyria handed to him by one of the Stalins, who then goes down to Ching Shih, strongly in the running for Most Valued Player right up until she reaches the semis and falls to a mutual fatal stabbing against La Quintrala.

It is perhaps the most entertaining thing I've seen since before the war. Zoe and I may between us have invented the best reality TV format known to mankind.

In the end there is only one of them left, and wouldn't you know it, it's Hitler. Basically because he's been hiding in a bunker all this time. He pokes his head up, and I set Miffly on him. Zoe and I have a fine old hoot watching Hitler get chased round and round a field by an allosaur. It's very therapeutic. And the thing about allosaurs is they can run really quite fast, and the thing about Hitlers is that they can't, not really, or not for very long.

As Miffly tucks in, I'm still snickering about the whole

wretched show of it. So is Zoe.

"We should do this again some time," I suggest.

"There are always more Hitlers," she agrees.

There is an awkward pause.

"This isn't what I thought you'd be like," she says, eventually, warily, still that distance between us that I'm more than happy with. "The Founder. Grandfather. I mean, aside from the overtones of incest in the whole thing. I thought you were going to be, you know, *nice*."

"Well, when I saw you, I assumed you'd be just another Smantha, all that gushing sincerity. I thought you'd be desperate to make sure your own society arose."

"I thought you'd just be desperate to get your end away, frankly," she says, with some disgust. "Living out here at the end of time, last man on the desert island of history. The way they teach it where I come from, you've got blue balls the size of Mercury before the Bride of the Founder comes along. And of course I didn't know that was going to be *me* when I was growing up, but I still thought it was gross. Everyone else thought it was 'romantic.'"

"Not if you were the last woman on Earth," I tell her, heartfelt. "And even if I was that desperate, one look at the place you come from would prompt me to a vow of celibacy. Besides, I know plenty of places to go for a good time. The whole of history's my brothel."

"Huh. They don't teach that bit at school," she admits. "So..." A philosophical pause where she rewrites the textbooks in her head. "I guess we go back to killing each other now?"

"We could do." I don't feel terribly keen on it, to be honest. You know how it is, you've tried all the positions, gone through all the kinks and quirks to try and keep things fresh. Eventually you just get jaded, though. I could keep trying to kill her for the rest of time, but I'd just be repeating myself.

She rubs at her chin. "We could, you know, take it as read that that's what we're doing." She looks over the field. "Assume, as a baseline, that you're doing your best to kill me and I'm doing my best to kill you. So we're cancelling each other out. Only, it's honestly taking up a lot of my time that I'd be happy to free up for other things."

"I need to get the harvest in," I agree. "Or at least nominally oversee the robots. It's difficult, what with constantly having to spend time trying to kill you. And avoiding being killed. It becomes a bit of a chore, eventually."

"Truce?"

"Truce," I agree. "Although obviously with no promises or anything. I am, after all, a very bad person and may turn on you at any moment."

"Ditto and likewise."

We relax a bit. Miffly lopes over, panting, and we take turns scratching her under the chin.

CHAPTER NINE

I WILL CONFESS we have a bit of a trust problem at first, what with all the trying-to-kill-each-other so fresh in both our minds. We spend the next few days out of each other's sight, waiting to see who will break the truce first. And I spy on her, and doubtless she spies on me. I have drones scouring the farm for her camps. I get up in the morning to find the crockery from her early breakfast still in the sink, and Miffly has a new collar that says *I had a blast at Pompeii* in Latin, a memento of a short-lived tourist board more prophetic than profitable.

And no scorpions in my shoes, and the suite of detectors I employ find nothing more dangerous than too much caffeine in my coffee. And if Zoe's going to kill me with over-caffeination then she's reckoned without the colossal tolerance I've already built up over an indeterminate lifetime of making it so strong the spoon stands up in it. And, for my part, I note the opportunities where I could unleash the hounds on her or launch a missile keyed to her genetic code, and I virtuously abstain, all the while knowing that the cold war could go hot the next day. And, just as with the time machines in the Causality War, whoever strikes first might just have an insuperable advantage.

And yet I stay my hand, and so does she, and after a week of that I send a cordial message by way of a white-flag-waving robot to suggest that, so long as she's mooching about the place, she might as well move into the farmhouse. It will give us a chance to keep an eye on each other, and it beats tents. I never could stand tents.

She sends me a message back, by way of a specially-trained genetically-engineered giant bee she was probably originally intending as an apiarian assassin, to say that actually she's been in the undercellar for the last few nights anyway, and the camps I've been staking out have been dummies. I reply, by way of a coded radio signal, *I have an undercellar?* and she tells me, by shouting quite loud up the stairs, that I'm so unperceptive it's amazing I lived long enough to enjoy this truce we're apparently having.

So it goes.

Soon after that, the alarms go off. For a moment I assume it's some of her compatriots come to check up on her, but instead it's three men in black suits and ties and sunglasses, turning up with a big machine of chrome and steel and glass and circuits, their armpits bulky with ill-concealed holsters.

Some sort of agency. Knowing their type, I'm all for giving them a taste of their own medicine and waterboarding a few confessions out of them, but Zoe has a better idea.

We hide all the robots and the dinosaurs and the rest of it, and when the Men In Black walk up to the farmhouse it's just the pair of us with no visible technology more sophisticated than the Soviet Speedster. We've even got ourselves up like American Gothic, pitchforks and puritan hats, and we make sure we talk with broad New England accents and act as though we've never seen anything so astoundingly futuristic as their mobile phones.

We act dumb. They ask us all manner of questions about how we got here, and we explain that we and the entire farm got vanished away from the good old U-S-of-A back in nineteen seventy-one by this great big flying saucer-looking thing, or maybe it was an angel or something, and we've been here ever since. What year is it? we demand of them. Who's the president? Ronald *who?* And the more we act the wide-eyed yokels, the more creeped-out they get, and they're Watching The Skies because the Truth Is Out There and Zoe and I are killing ourselves laughing and fighting like mad to keep a straight face every time they look at us.

And we listen in on their murmured conversations and their telephone calls until we know exactly what agency they represent, where their HQ is, what president they don't report to for reasons of plausible deniability and just how easy it would be to make their whole super-secret nobody-ever-heard-of-us organisation disappear without a trace. And then we sneak off and sabotage their time machine so it takes them back before the beginning of the universe. After that, we go in our own rather better time machine and fix a couple of elections and one funding debate, and their secret agency vanishes in a puff of congressional oversight, and that's one more threat to the fabric of reality dealt with.

Zoe and I kick back and relax that evening, on the couch, in front of the fire. I put the TV on. I've a specially curated selection of box sets, because one thing that spins like a weathervane when you change causality is entertainment, and if you have a deft hand you can collect all the really *good* versions of things, like the final series of *Lost* where all the loose ends actually got tied up, or that peculiarly tangled timeline where William Shakespeare, Helen Mirren and Orson Welles got together to make a *Transformers* movie.

"So that's what you do," Zoe says, after we've taken in a couple of shows.

"I preserve the future," I agree piously. "I lived through the Causality War, after all. I was there when they went from conventional apocalyptic weapons to time machines, and I was there when they went from time machines to the Causality Bombs. And never again. The rest of time must remain inviolate for all time. I can't allow anyone to start gadding about through the epochs. Not even your people. *Especially* not your people."

She nods slowly. "That's very virtuous of you."

"I thought so."

"It's not true, though."

I go still, waiting to see how problematic this conversation is going to be. "Oh?"

"I mean, I suppose that is *also* what you're doing," she allows graciously, and she is eyeing me sidelong just the same way I'm eyeing her. There's a definite space between us on the couch, and any moment we might both be leaping up to take cover behind it, the truce in pieces on the floor. Which would mean we both end up hiding from each other on the same side of the couch, which might be strategically awkward, but one thing at a time.

"I'm really not sure what you mean," I say, unconvincing even to my own ears.

"You're not really trying to save the future," she says. "You've set up here, on the first piece of historical real estate to survive what the war did, at the start of the rest of history. You've turned it into your own perfect eternal day on the shores of forever. You've made sure nobody can travel past you. Like you keep saying, they all end up here. And you kill them, all of them. Just like you did your best with me." And she waves away my protests: she's not accusing me. Or she *is* accusing me, technically, but not actually faulting me. "But it's not because you want to preserve time. It's because you're a misanthropic bastard who just really enjoys being the last surviving human being. You've gone to live like a hermit on a desert island, only the desert island's the whole of the rest of history, and you can't abide sharing it with anyone."

I stare at the blank screen for a bit. "And?"

"Your turn to talk now."

"I was in the war," I say.

"You keep saying."

"I was a soldier. That means doing what you're told. Very

keen on that, in the army. And because it was a war across time, and because every time anyone from either side went back in time to change things, everything *else* changed too, the people telling me what to do kept changing. Who they were, what they represented, most especially what their orders were. I'd go do a hatchet job on history to bring something about, and then my new chain of command would be telling me to go do the precise opposite, to restore the way things were, only of course they didn't realise that was what they were asking me to do. Because they had no memory of the way things had been originally. And eventually neither did I, because I'd seen so many versions of my own present day that I couldn't remember how it had been. And each time there was someone telling me that it was vitally important for the future of the nation, or the war, or the world, that I go back in time and make this change or that. And I wanted to tell them that it *couldn't* be that important, because we'd already done it, and undone it, and done it differently, and a thousand variations in between. Me and my fellow time soldiers and all our opposite numbers, over and over.

"And we died, we time soldiers. We killed each other and got eaten by dinosaurs and our time machines imploded and... just death, really. And though there were fewer and fewer of us, we were meddling more and more, and eventually I ended up in a staff meeting where seventy-five per cent of the people were actually me, from various points in my career. The longer I stayed in service, the more of the whole mess I was personally ending up responsible for. It was insane, just insane. And, of course, somewhere in there I worked out that the only person I could possibly trust or obey or listen to was me. Every other human being was just like a shape made of fog, gone the moment you turn away. Because when you're travelling through time you're the only constant. It's not even stepping on a butterfly. Go into the past and breathe a mouthful of air, intercept a handful of photons, you've changed the world in ways you can't possibly predict."

I have literally never had the chance to get this off my chest before. I didn't even realise catharsis was something I needed.

"And so... Well, then they started with the bombs, of course. I became a time bombardier, or some of me did. Because high command—all the high commands, for a given value of both height and command, given they kept changing—worked out that time was mutable, and just started detonating points in history, trying to make firebreaks so that earlier changes couldn't affect later eras. And that led to a chain reaction that turned a century either side of my birth into sand and the rest of history leading up to that point into disconnected chunks of various durations. And almost nobody survived. Except quite a lot of people survived, escaping ground zero in a variety of time engines and skulking about bits of history, some of them still fighting the war, some of them hunting each other. Some of them just trying to stay alive.

"And I made sure that none of them did. I got rid of them. Because by then I knew I couldn't share a continuum with even one other time-travel-capable human being. Not one.

Because I needed things to stop changing. I needed the merry-go-round to stop. Stability, Zoe. And give a mouse a time machine and he'll screw over history over and over and you won't know what year it is or who's president. And so I made my rule. No time machines. Not on my watch. And my watch is going on forever."

She nods, giving me the side-eye. "You're a misanthropic bastard," she summarises.

"Yes. I mean, I'm trying to plead mitigating circumstances here, but that is what it boils down to. I'm bad at sharing things, up to and including existence."

Another pause, and then she says, "Well, I'm flattered, then. That this truce is lasting."

And I have a think about that, and about Hitler getting chased about a muddy field by Miffly, and about playing the slack-jawed yokel for the Men In Black, and come to the remarkable revelation that I didn't actually mind having someone to share the fun with.

We watch the really *good* cut of the *Princess Bride* next, the one that's even better than the one you got to see, and then we say our farewells, me for my bedroom and she for her den in the undercellar that apparently my farmhouse has. "Goodnight," we say, and then we both come in with, "I'll most likely kill you in the morning," and we laugh, because it's probably true. And yet, when the morning comes, we don't.

I FEEL THAT, as history's most experienced living time

traveller, I should explain to her some great deep secret of the trade. She is, after all, both new to this and an absolute natural hand at it (although, with time travel, you can go from new to an accomplished master in the blink of someone else's subjective eye).

I feel that I should take her under my wing and make her my apprentice, have her shuffle about in my footsteps as I drone on about equations and consequences and the dire responsibility of preserving the timeline. Except that ship has sailed, caught fire, sunk and then been eaten by a megalodon. Instead, the secret of secrets that bubbles up from within me is, "Time travel is really fun."

"One more reason to keep it for yourself, eh?"

"Well, yes. Because, believe me, the more people who are doing it, the less fun it gets. But if there's just one of you... Or two, even. In fact, I've been thinking, and there are some things that we might do together. If you're up for it."

Zoe gives me the arched eyebrow. "Sounds kinky to me."

"It is," I agree, "a very particular kink."

We go back to the early Bronze Age and see who can pull the best fake miracles on Old Testament prophet types, resulting in a veritable plague of boggle-eyed loons deserting their flocks to preach new and unlikely commandments to increasingly impatient Levantine tribes. We drop in on the Cretaceous and race dinosaurs against each other, winner eats the loser. We steal fistfuls of mutagens from some pre-war bioweapons program and then go back five hundred million years to mess with early life, see who can make the Cambrian explosion go with the biggest bang. I end up making a pink newt-looking thing twelve feet long with a back covered with ostrich-feathers and eyes on eight foot stalks. We christen it *Herpaderpus* and decide it's the winner.

We pick some wars and put on generals' hats. I win Borodino against Zoe's Napoleon after mounting all the Russians on dire wolves. She obliterates my plucky British at Rourke's Drift by giving the Zulus a couple of tanks. We fight the Battle of Zhizhi to a standstill after both claimants to the Chinese throne inherit a squad of US Marines, some woolly rhinos and a fleet of hovercraft. After that, with bloodlust more than slaked, we compete to see who can successfully introduce twenty-first century reality TV concepts to the classical world, which Zoe wins with *I'm A Caligula, Get Me Out Of Here.*

I mean, I could have done these things on my own, you understand. I have always been perfectly capable of amusing myself.

(And it wasn't as though, when there were any of my peers from the Causality War still around, they'd have been up for this kind of hijinks. They took the business of ruining history for everyone very seriously. And why? No dogma, no nation, no cultural identity and no ideology survived the war intact. Within the first weeks of history being written and rewritten, there was literally nothing to fight for. And yet they kept on fighting, because to stop would be to admit we should never have started. History was brought down by a colossal investment in the sunk cost fallacy.)

But Zoe *gets it.* Zoe understands the essential meaninglessness of history now it's lying in pieces on the floor. It might have been your Aunt's priceless vase a moment ago, but now it's been elbowed off the side-table, it's just bits. And nobody cares what you do with bits.

All those lives, you say? Are you going to go to bat once more for all that grandeur, the spectacle, the knowledge, the great sweeping breadth of human achievement? It's on the floor now. King's horses, king's men, right? And if we go to some piece of it or other and fundamentally mess up the sequence of events, get a million people killed, exterminate some species, obliterate a continent in an orbital railgun barrage... It doesn't actually matter any more. It doesn't change anything. It's just one fragment of vase on the floor of time.

And I'm waiting for her to get cold feet, I guess. I'm waiting for her to look upon my works, ye mighty, and say, hold on, maybe this is all a bit cruel, a bit selfish. But she doesn't She's game for anything, is Zoe. And with her, it's twice as much fun to trample the broken vase. Who'd have ever thought I'd find a soulmate in the end times? Not me, obviously, what with my trying my damnedest to eliminate the rest of the human race.

ONE MORNING AFTER we're back, the alarm goes off again. We had a heavy night, having gone on a colossal bender across half of time and space, so I'm uncharacteristically slow to get out of bed. Zoe has a more robust constitution, and by the time I slope over, she's already located the latest batch of errant time travellers.

It's not the usual. I recognise the voices even as I shamble over. It's Smantha and Weldon.

I go cold. *Surely she hasn't…?* But it seems all too likely, in the cold and hungover light of morning. After all, it's her entire civilization at stake. Why shouldn't she play along with a selfish old bastard like me?

They're in a copse off by the top field and I creep over, hiding myself behind a tree to eavesdrop, because sometimes all the high-tech surveillance gear in the world isn't immediate enough for you.

"What are you doing, Zoe?" Smantha is demanding of her. "You're supposed to have settled down, already."

"We're getting worried, back home," Weldon adds. "Look, I've brought some graphs."

He has, as well. He's always looked exactly like the sort of tedious wanker who'd bring out graphs, and now he's doing it. All the fancy holographic projection his perfect Utopia can muster can't make this sort of nonsense engaging, but he obviously feels he's God's own gift to every middle management meeting. "The probability curve is declining alarmingly," he announces, as though everyone is supposed to leap up and cry, "Oh, no!"

"We're honestly not sure what you've been doing, Zoe," Smantha says. "But can you just get on and start having children like you're supposed to. You know, like you actually *did* in our past. I'm sure it's hard living in these primitive surroundings with him, but just pull your weight for once, will you?"

"I have a flowchart, too," Weldon adds helpfully.

"I understand," Zoe says, a bit hastily because he doubtless really does have a flowchart and he's not afraid to use it. "You're concerned."

"We are a bit worried that things don't seem to actually be moving towards the correct sequence of events, yes," confirms Weldon. I wait for him to pull out a motivational poster, but even he isn't that much of a monster.

"So if you could, you know, just get it done," Smantha puts in. "I mean, once the next generation's secure, you can come back. We'll take it from there."

"Uh-huh," Zoe says, and I lean in to hear just how she's going to put the knife in. And it's a shame. I really have had fun, these last few weeks. But I suppose it's back to murdering each other again, and while that has its own appeal, it just won't be the same.

And then she says, "Go to hell, though."

"Excuse me, what?" Weldon looks put out, as though ending up in hell is a node he missed off the flowchart.

"Screw the lot of you," Zoe says. "I'm not doing it."

There's a pause, in which I assume the two Utopians exchange perfect glances.

"But... we need you to," Weldon says.

"You *have* to," Smantha says, more forcefully. "Otherwise none of it happens. Otherwise there's no *us*, any of us. Your parents, everyone you knew, our entire civilization, Zoe. I mean, how selfish can you be?"

"Precisely this selfish," Zoe tells them. "Because nobody ever asked *me*, and because every one of you has been telling me how I have to sacrifice myself for the greater good so you can go on having your lovely comfortable lives, and you know what? I don't, actually." I can picture her smiling, I really can. "So you just get going, the pair of you. Go back home while there's still a home and while there's still a you. And if you show your faces round here again, I'll set Miffly on you."

And I feel my heart grow three sizes, because she's a bitter sociopath, but she's *my* bitter sociopath.

That night, we're sitting together watching that weird *Casablanca* sequel starring Rick Astley that turned out so unexpectedly well, and I decide it's time I grew a pair and made the appropriate gesture.

"I heard what you said, earlier," I confirm, and she nods, watching me warily.

"Only," I go on, "if you wanted... I should make clear *I* don't actually want this, but... if *you* wanted, then I'd do it, for you. Only for you." I take a deep breath. It's a hard thing to commit to. "But if you wanted, I'd be willing to settle down and have a utopia."

She grins. "You'd do that for me?"

The words are out, now. I'm committed. "If you wanted."

"Well I don't," she reassures me. "But that's sweet of you. It's nice to know."

CHAPTER TEN

WHAT HAPPENS NEXT is that they turn their attention to me. I'm off ploughing the top field for the next crop of sprouts when Weldon turns up. He's made an effort: he's riding a twenty-third-century hover tractor and he's got dungarees on, and even a straw hat of the kind I favour, except he wears it really badly. He looks like he's on his way to the dullest ever costume party.

"Howdy, neighbour!" he hails me, full of fake cheer. "Looks like a… bumper crop of… something, this year."

"Sprouts," I tell him.

Coming from a utopia, of course, he has no idea what sprouts are.

"Listen, I wanted to have a manly talk with you, man to man, as men," he explains heartily. "Only, it looks like there's one... field on your farm that you haven't... ploughed, so to speak, if you see what I mean." Having vomited up the laboured innuendo, he makes a grotesque show of waggling his eyebrows.

"Weldon," I tell him reasonably, "get in the sea."

"No, but listen," he says desperately. "There's a lot riding on this, and it's not as if we're asking much. You might even enjoy it. It's not so much to ask."

"She doesn't want to. And I don't want to. We're getting along platonically just exactly fine." Meaning we spent all afternoon throwing things at Plato and it was hilarious. "So you can just go back to your perfect future and cease to exist, if you please."

"No, look," Weldon insists. "You have no idea what's at stake. This is so much bigger than you."

I stop the Soviet Speedster and lean on the steering wheel, looking at him. "I understand exactly what's at stake. I am the time travel veteran. I've seen whole chains of human historical events come and go as we fought over time. And then I saw the bombs fall and everything there ever was get splintered into pieces forever. And your lot, your precious perfect art deco society? It's not all that, mate. It's not the topless towers of Ilium. I won't miss it, when it's gone. When it never was. Because that's the point with things that get erased from the future: you *don't* miss them, by definition. Now off you trot. Go make a pie-chart or something."

But he doesn't get in the temporal sea and nor does Smantha. Over the next week at the farm, we're constantly running into the pair of them. They keep trying to pretend that it's all chance meetings and *Oh, what were the odds of running into you two here?* which, given this is where we live and we are literally the only people in the entirety of the world at this point in time, wears a bit thin fairly quickly. And they keep doing this whole false-jolly routine of asking how we're getting on and is there any big news we want to share, all of that. And you can see the strain at the corners of their smiles, but that doesn't make it any less annoying. I think I've finally found a situation where someone else's discomfort isn't actually funny.

So Zoe and I go for another holiday to get away from it, a gadabout around the rough terrain of history, tweaking famous noses and playing God for the people in the cheap seats. Except now we can't get away from them. We lose ourselves in the crowds at the Coliseum, and who should be on the bench behind us talking in loud voices about what a lovely couple we make but Weldon and Smantha. We descend into the fleshpots of nineteenth-century Paris and in the very tawdry brothel we settle on, the pair of them are already ensconced and booking us a private room with the bawd. On the deserted section of Devonian beach we choose for a stroll, someone's set out a romantic table for two with some wine and oysters. Or, if not actually oysters, some kind of primeval mollusc.

It takes all the fun out of it. What was previously just a carefree spree of mayhem and chaos carved through the corpse of history now feels like a holiday with your prurient maiden aunt. Except in this case Auntie is desperate for us to get it on, and it's really, really off-putting. Everywhere we go, every time period, every version of the timeframe, there they are: making encouraging faces, playing inexpert mood music, coining laborious double entendres (or, as they get steadily more desperate, single entendres).

Zoe and I seriously discuss actually doing it to get them off our backs—by which I mean murdering Weldon and Smantha. Except their goddamn hangdog expressions, the passive-aggressive accusing looks we keep getting from them, it's all a bit too much. *You can kill us,* those looks seem to say, *but just save our world!* and it's no fun. It must have been this way for Roman Emperors and barbarian warlords when confronted with actual saintly martyrs. I mean, when they're begging you to tie them up and throw them on a fire, the whole business rather loses its fun factor.

We even try to fake them out by going back to the farmhouse and making a big fuss about getting our jollies on as noisily as possible in the hope they'll be satisfied and leave us alone. We go at it hammer and tongs in a variety of locations and positions, using, of course, every contraceptive method known to man because we really don't want to be engendering any little utopias. Except Weldon and Smantha are on the case and they're not to be put off by anything quite so theatrical. They keep turning up with pregnancy tests and Weldon's damnable graphs, and it's obvious that a little physical intimacy won't put them off. By that time they're so intrusive that there are frequently two or three *sets* of Weldons and Smanthas hanging around the farm at any one time, and it's frankly intolerable.

One evening, Zoe pops the pertinent question. We've closed the curtains and barred the doors against them, but it doesn't help. By then we're almost supernaturally *aware* of Weldons and Smanthas. We know they're there, noses pressed to the glass like urchins at a pie shoppe window, And she asks. "How long, exactly? I mean, we absolutely have not given rise to their future. Shouldn't they have popped out of existence by now?"

"Well that's the tricky thing about time and causality," I admit. And then I have to make the much more painful admission that, "It's all in Weldon's bloody graphs, really. There's a waveform of probability that leads to them. When it's zero, that's when there will never have been a Weldon and a Smantha and all the bloody lot of it. If I killed you, or you killed me, that would do it. But as we're both still about, the probability is obviously sufficiently this side of zero that their future is still clinging on." I sigh. "And, depressingly enough, even if it went, the whole of the past is lousy with Weldons and Smanthas now. Even if their originating timeframe didn't happen, *they'd* still be around because when you travel in time you sever yourself from causality. My own past is a blank slate; I'm the product of a whole snarl of timelines that all never happened."

"So we'll never be rid of them, even after the universe accepts that we're not going to play mum and dad to their society?" Zoe demands in exasperation.

"Well, my plan was, once that actually happened and the supply of new Weldons and Smanthas definitively dried up, we could hunt them for sport," I suggested. "No point now, because we'd just keep getting more, but when they're actually an endangered species, we could wipe them out. In fact we'd have to, because we—"

"Can't have time travellers running about ruining the place," Zoe agrees. "But I'd rather the universe got its act together and accepted we aren't going to do the dirty. Because they are getting right on my tits."

"Let's go on another trip," I suggest.

"Is it worth it? They're always *there*. I can't just kick back and relax when they're looking over my shoulder all the time."

"I've thought of somewhere they shouldn't be. And it's somewhere I was thinking of showing you. Somewhere special."

She looks at me narrowly, because one of things when you have the whole of time and space to visit is that nowhere is really *special*. There's so much wonder that it's all a bit samey, after a while. Except there is somewhere.

I never go there. Or *then*. I don't make the journey, as a rule. It's not actually a happy place. It has a personal resonance for me that's somewhat downbeat. But it's beautiful, in a terrible way, and Zoe should see it.

I take her to the edge of the war.

We broke time, like I said. In the last throes of the war every remaining faction simultaneously developed an *ultimate* ultimate weapon, after discovering that mere time machines reshaping history wasn't ultimate enough. Everyone had the Causality Bomb and, just as with time machines, everyone agreed not to use them. And then they used them, because that's what you always do with the ultimate weapons that you swear you'll never, ever use. You get your retaliation in first. Sooner or later, you pre-emptively deploy your deterrent just in case the other side aren't deterred by it.

And time got cut into chunks, as you've seen, but around the period of the actual war itself—that century or two that would have contained all the moments and days of my actual personal history—that was ground zero. That took the brunt of the blast.

"What," Zoe asks, "am I looking at?"

Normally you can't see into time, because photons don't work like that, and nor do human brains. You have to do something pretty damn stupid and spectacular to reduce the actual structure of time to something you can sit there and look at.

I've brought a picnic and a tartan blanket and a couple of deck chairs, and we're sitting on the shores of time, where the big chunks of moments get progressively smaller until it's like sand. Until it's just dust. Until, if you pick your vantage point very carefully, you can pop open a cold one and look into forever, where fractions of a murdered second shimmer like a heat haze on the horizon. Where the receding last moments of the war stretch out like glittering rainbow sand into an infinite perspective, and here and there a chunk of time like a beached iceberg standing proud of the rest. It's an eye-twisting, brain-bending sight. It's beauty like a black hole is beautiful. It's staring the impossible in the face, the wreck of things that shouldn't even be made manifest in the first place, let alone be destroyed.

In short, I've taken Zoe back home, though she won't be meeting the family. I don't even remember the family. They were an early casualty of the war, unwritten from time along with everything else while I was off playing soldier.

We sit there sombrely and sip our beers. It is not a fun place. We won't be playing any pranks or holding dumb contests here. It's not a place for jokes.

"Damn," she says after a while, and I nod agreement.

You can see my house from here, I want to tell her. But you can't and it's not true and there never was a house and it's all just powdered time crunching underfoot; fragments of chronology too small to ever visit. Everything I ever was, everything that led to me, all the times of my lives.

And I'm not saying this is why I'm the bastard I am. I own to my bastardy. But at the same time, this is what makes me a literal temporal bastard, as well as orphan. Nothing more illegitimate than a man whose grandfather got killed before meeting his grandmother, and at this remove I can't even remember if it was me who did it.

At least, though, this frozen moment of funereal solitude should give us some respite from bloody Weldon and Smantha.

Except...

"Isn't that...?" Zoe says, peering into the non-distance.

"What?"

"There, near that big chunk of... Wednesday. Something's moving."

I squint, shading my eyes from the glare of fourth-dimensional devastation. Out there across the scintillating desert, out by one of the bigger pieces of beached time, something's moving. Two somethings. Two dreadfully familiar somethings.

They were, I think, trying to be subtle for once, but they stop when they realise we've spotted them. Weldon and Smantha, the scourge of the space-time continuum.

I think they're going to saunter over, then. I'm fully braced for a hearty hail-fellow-well-met-fancy-meeting-you-here from them, followed by the usual nudge-nudge-wink-wink-how-are-you-two-lovebirds nonsense they usually come up with. Mercifully, though, they just look furtive and skedaddle, receding into the vanishing point of history as quickly as their toes can take them. But they were here, and that's enough to ruin the moment.

In the aftermath of that I give a great sigh.

"I think we're going to have to do something drastic," I say, and Zoe nods philosophically.

"I don't think we can just wait for them to never have existed," she agrees.

It's not something I ever thought I'd countenance. It's basically the antithesis of every vow I ever made, in fact. But right now, we are going to have to cross some lines if we ever want to enjoy some peace and quiet without the temporal neighbours dropping round.

CHAPTER ELEVEN

"How hard will it be," Zoe asks, "to start from scratch?"

We're both on the Speedster, taking one last turn around the farm, Miffly mooching alongside. Zoe's behind me, sidesaddle, one leg up to her chin as we jolt along, a hand on my shoulder for stability. It's amazing how used to her I am. Honestly, we were trying to kill each other not very long ago at all, and now I can't imagine eternity without her.

And we'll probably get bored of one another sooner or later, and then it'll be her or me again, sure enough. But I can't find even the seeds of that in me, and I hope it's the same for her. And if I do end up killing her, I know I'll regret it sooner or later and those regrets will last forever. So perhaps we can just agree to spend an eon or two apart and then get back together. Perhaps, after all, we'll just be civilized about it and won't actually need to kill each other at all.

Perhaps this final act of barbarism will teach us to be good from hereon in.

"If any of this survives, we can just plunder it for what we want to keep," I say. I don't know if it will, though. What I'm planning isn't an exact science.

We go out to a hilltop where the whole farm is spread out below us. I can see my house from here, the one I built with my own hands. Also a buttload of robots, but I was at least involved in the process. I can see the wheatfields and the turnips and the cabbages and the golden glory of the sunflowers. The sheep like little clouds on the hillside across the way. And it's never going to be the same, not any more. It won't be home. Just another piece on the floor, if it survives at all.

Because the constant intrusions of Smantha and Weldon have got too much for me. I'm countenancing the unthinkable. And it will be profoundly inconvenient, to have to rebuild elsewhere and elsewhen. But I did it before, and this time there will be two of us. Many hands make light work, and that's even truer when you've raided the past for as many robots as you need.

"All right, then," Zoe says. "How do we go about this?"

With difficulty, is the answer to that. With a lot of careful prep. With a sense of finality. This isn't something you can just *do*. The only reason our destination still exists is that it's very secret and very hard to reach and extremely inhospitable to any kind of life that requires a regular space-time frame of reference, which is to say all life. Including Zoe and me, so we have to take precautions and get some very special protective clothing.

It's not easy to invent kit that will protect you from the dreadful effects of collapsing time, but it was something of a priority right towards the end of the war. And as a rule all that kit turned out not to be quite effective enough, and it was obliterated into non-existence along with all the time-space volumes that contained it when the boom went up and causality went boom. But I'd snuck some out, by then. I'd taken some of that gear and hidden it in 1192 Byzantium, in a place and time that now exists as a loop of four hours ninety-seven minutes out there in the rubble of history. And then, when the dust had cleared and I'd made myself my new home, I took it and stuck it in the farmhouse's attic with all the other junk I thought I'd never need again.

We lay it out on the kitchen table. Chronic baffles, tachyon screeds, vortex dampeners, boson filtration tubes. All that cumbersome nonsense people were loading themselves up with at the end. And none of it would protect you from the blast of a Causality Bomb, in the same way as a hazmat suit wouldn't let you walk slowly away from a nuclear explosion like an action hero in one of those movies. Although, if you were an action hero in a movie, you'd have the hood of the hazmat suit off so the audience could see your chiselled features, and so it would be even less use than that.

We load up with the gear. I saved enough stuff for about three people. I have no idea who the other two people were that I was intending to kit out. Probably they got erased from time so thoroughly that even my memories of them got wiped. That gives me a disquieting moment of self-reflection. *Had* there been someone, back then? When I had the idea of building the farm out on the edge of forever, was it really just for me?

And the grim answer, the one I always give to myself when these thoughts occur to me: it doesn't matter. I can't remember, and if it's gone from my memory, then it's gone from the universe. The only thing that matters is the here and now. Literally.

"Happy with what we're doing?" I ask, after we've got the gear on and are waddling off towards our time machines.

"Fifty-eight seconds!" So muffled by her helmet I can barely hear her. We're on the same page, though. That's how long we'll have. That's how long our target shard of time lasts. In and out in under a minute, the perfect heist.

Because it's out there. One shard of time I saw once and marked with an X on my secret causality map. My secret. The big one. Fifty-eight seconds of war that survived the blast intact. And maybe it's fifty-eight seconds of my own actual past, but I can't remember, and so that's that. It's there, is all. And I've lived with the knowledge of it for... well, for an indeterminate amount of time, things being how they are. And I know I should have destroyed it. It's far too dangerous to leave lying about. But every time I tried to, a little voice in my head said, *You might need it. You never know.* And you know what? That little voice was right.

And now it's time to raid the piggy bank. Zoe and I are

going back to the war for a souvenir.

I remember when it all went to hell, during the war. A mad scramble to do unto them before they did unto us. Not the constant back and forth of the time machines—which by then, it was clear, wasn't solving anything—but the ultimate of ultimates, that it was utterly crucial *we* deploy *first*. Except it was a war in time, and so terms like 'before' and 'first' didn't hold the absolute meaning people usually ascribed to them. And it all went off at once. And you've seen how that turned out for poor old history, greatest of all civilian casualties.

I don't know how many Causality Bombs there were. I suspect even one would have been too many and there were certainly more than one. And for every bomb there was a team tasked with deploying it, detonating it on a precise fault-line of history so that some key part of *their* game plan or culture or hierarchy would just get atomised, the whole spacetime proximity just blasted into four-dimensional powder. Imagine them, all those squads of determined soldiers, all of the time-orphans, products of sequences of events, places, parents, times now hopelessly overwritten in the shifting chaos of the war. Picture them in their vastly cumbersome suits of protective gear that would not under any circumstances protect them. They're there, crouching around the ludicrous complexity of their particular bomb, however it might look. They all looked different: brass and clockwork, crystal, lead, moving parts, funnels, wires. None of them looked entirely physical. They hurt the eyes. I remember.

And they set off the bombs. I remember. Crouching, encumbered, each alone in that great swaddling suit. Detonating the present, burning the past. Because it was a war that had no justification any more and there was no other way of ending it except to end everything else and hope the war got caught in the blast.

I remember.

And we were there—or *they* were there, if it turns out it wasn't me at all—at the bomb, just as all the other teams were there with their bombs. Except that someone, one of our and/or their team, had a quirk of conscience. Just a moment when they thought, *We shouldn't do this, though*. Just a brief second of second thoughts. But it was a time war, and a brief second is all it takes to fall out of step with the rest of the conflict. So that, when it all went kaboom, this one bomb wasn't ready and didn't go off. And didn't matter, as it turned out, because there were enough bombs being detonated in that same second to wipe out history several times over. But that bomb, that one bomb, didn't go bang. And that bomb, and its hesitating team, and its moment of conscience, ended up stuck in a shard fifty-eight seconds long, and it's still out there. The last Causality Bomb in causality. And Zoe and I are going to go get it, and we'll take it to Smantha and Weldon's perfect paradise. Perhaps we'll gift-wrap it for them.

We'll detonate it and turn their entire postepochalyptic utopia into a wasteland of nothing, and then we'll go build a new farm on the new broken edge of history, whenever that turns out to be, and settle down to murder time travellers and troll historical figures again. Everyone should have a retirement plan.

We synchronise our time machines. It's like synchronising watches, only considerably more complicated. Our in-and-out window is less than a minute, after all. Precision beyond the dreams of the Swiss is the watchword.

We depart.

We arrive. The journey is instantaneous. It's time travel. The travel part doesn't take any time. Obviously some sort of dramatic falling-through-space-into-a-swirly-vortex sort of thing would be narratively preferable, but it is what it is.

And then we're raising the hatches, clumsy in our layers of protection, lumbering out into the moments before history exploded. It's a warehouse, I think. There's a terrible glare coming in from somewhere that isn't really any regular direction. It's not the ghastly light of the detonated Causality Bombs, because when they went off they took light with them along with everything else. Even light is a slave to cause and effect, and once you cut those strings the puppet falls on the floor and ceases to be particularly entertaining. But it's something like that. Not the explosion, but the *pre*splosion. It's the light of the Armageddon about to happen. When you blow up time, you see the mushroom cloud before the bomb goes off. I mean, that's only common sense, right?

And up ahead, barely visible in the eye-watering light, we see five figures. The bomb squad, sexless, featureless in the same heavy gear we're wearing, kneeling in a circle. And I remember.

I don't remember.

I don't know if I remember.

I've been here multiple times before, after all, and my actual recollection of the late moments of the war is like confetti. Five figures, and am I one of them? How would that even work, that I'm here revisiting the scene of my maybe epiphany, if I never actually left? Maybe I leave later, on the fifty-eighth second. But the other thing about everyone else setting off their space-time-shredding ultimate weapons is that it plays hob with your memory for a few days before and after the event. And as the event encompasses all of time, well...

So maybe one of them's me, and maybe I already left. And maybe I was the one who had the crisis of conscience and didn't detonate this, the last of the Causality Bombs. Or maybe it was someone else. I kind of hope the latter is the case because otherwise I am about to trample all over my former scruples.

We shamble forwards, feeling the seconds dropping behind us like lead weights. I can see our armour ablating away under the sheer corrosive pressure of burning time, the blast wave that moves backwards through history, the firework that blows up your pets in the house before you even light the blue touch paper.

We get to those five frozen figures. From a direction known only to the fourth dimension, the end of all things is rolling towards us.

There's no bomb.

No bomb.

There's no bomb.

I mean, we spend some vital seconds looking for it, but there's no bomb.

How can there be no bomb? It's an ultimate weapon; it's not like it'll have rolled under the couch or it's in someone's other pair of jeans.

There's even a little round clear spot on the ground, the nothing that these five doomed sods are gathered around. But we're too late. Somebody already came and took it.

CHAPTER TWELVE

WE GO BACK to the farm, understandably dispirited. Disquieted, even, and given the whole reason for settling down on the farm was for a bit of quiet, that is entirely unsatisfactory. But if you stash an ultimate weapon somewhere and then you go back for it and someone's already nicked off with it, then that is a reasonable basis for a bit of disquiet.

Back at the farm, something's different.

It's hard to pinpoint. Everything is where we left it. Miffly bounds up wanting a scratch and maybe an errant time traveller to nibble on. The corn's just ripening, ready for me to take the tarpaulin off a harvester and go chug through the fields feeling like a proper son of the soil. Or else just leave it to the robots. Whatever. Except when I get out of my time machine and set my feet on the good dark earth, it feels... fragile. It feels as though there's a great hollow cavern below, and I can distantly hear the echo of every footfall. As if it could all collapse any moment.

Zoe doesn't quite get the same sense of it, but then I've been here longer. I've just generally been around the spacetime block longer. You develop senses.

"Well, I suppose we'd better..." I don't really know what we'd better, given how things have turned out. We need a new plan, anyway. Maybe if the Utopians are going to come here and bug us, we can go to their perfect world and graffiti their nice white walls, scratch all their silver trim, teach their beautiful, flawless children bad words. I mean, if in doubt, just generally screw up the world for everyone else, right? That's been the motto of human decision-making since Ug first hit Throg in the head with a rock, and it always seems to have gotten us through. Except for the whole Causality War and breaking everything there ever was into a million billion pieces, of course.

Smantha and Weldon are waiting for us outside the farmhouse. I wonder for a moment if we should pretend we had it away to our heart's content off in the past and stashed our kid, their sainted ancestor, in some random piece of history. A reed basket or a handbag or a left luggage locker or something. Then they can go hunting all space and time for the entirely fictitious mite and we can have a bit of peace and quiet.

But there's an odd look to the pair of them. They're not doing the strained-smiles and eager-beaver how's-the-family nonsense they usually resort to. They're actually looking a bit serious and I think I like them even less.

"We know where you were, by the way," Weldon starts. "Looking for the bomb."

"I don't know anything about any bomb," I say brightly. "How about you, darling? Did you happen to see a bomb?"

"I did not, love. No bombs at all," Zoe replies, likewise. And that is, of course, a sore point because a lack of bomb is precisely our problem, but tweaking these two's sanctimonious noses takes the edge off a little.

Smantha and Weldon exchange a little look. And, though I didn't like them when they were being jolly and earnest, and I didn't like them when they weren't, I like that little look even less.

The penny drops a moment after. Zoe goes tense right at the same time, making the equivalent connection. I remember when we went out to the beach on the edge of eternity, looking out-into-across-through that desert of shattered time. They'd been there, Smantha and Weldon, and for once they hadn't wanted to come over and badger us. Sneaking, almost. Like they'd been caught looking for something.

"You took the bomb," I say hollowly. "The last Causality Bomb. The only one to survive the war. You got in ahead of us and took it." Raiding that little fifty-eight second span of time, treading mere moments ahead of us so that we walked all unknowing in their footsteps, taking the bomb and stealing away just a breath before we were there to steal the same thing.

"We did, yes," Smantha says. "And just as well we did. We know exactly what you'd have done with it."

I favour them with a sour look. "Well, bully for you, you found us out," I say.

"But there'll be a next time," Zoe backs me up. "We'll find something else. And even if we don't, we don't lead to you anymore. We're quite happy without kids, thank you very much. And I appreciate that you, as the kids of the kids of the kids we're not going to have, are a bit aggrieved by that, but screw you, frankly."

"Even though you yourself are a product of that union you're so determined not to have," Smantha challenges her bitterly.

"Meh, I'm outside the timestream now. Doesn't affect me if I never get born. You too, for that matter. Why not just accept it and find somewhere nice, and forget Utopia?"

"Because it's *Utopia!*" Weldon actually shouts. "It's the best place! That's what it means."

"Nope," I say rather smugly. "It literally means 'no-place.' So you could just say we're trying to help it reach its proper potential by making sure it never happens."

"And just because it's Utopia for *you* doesn't mean it was to me," Zoe points out. "Or what about all those people who aren't around in that Utopia? Because it wouldn't have been for them either."

"We're not giving you the option any more," Weldon states flatly.

"You want my genetic material, you come here and take it," I tell him, ready for a bout of fisticuffs.

"We did consider it," he agrees. "But it just seemed too... messy. And not the way it was supposed to go, so who knows whether that would even give rise to *us*. You fought in the Causality War. You know that you can change a timeline as easily as that"—a snap of his fingers—"but it's basically impossible to ever go *back* to the original. You just get more and more different outcomes." And he's right, of course. "And that's why we took the bomb."

I'm still nodding about the lecture on causality that I almost miss that last bit. "Wait, that's why the what now?"

"You took the bomb to stop us using it," Zoe corrects him nervously.

"Actually," and now it's Smantha's turn to be smug, "we were looking for it long before you had the idea to get it."

"Impossible. How could you even know where it was?" And I'm getting tired of just standing out in front of the farmhouse like it's nigh noon, and so we all end up in the kitchen. With the kettle on and some little probably-not-poisoned crumpets out because I take my duties as host seriously even in these circumstances.

"We knew," Smantha says, once I've poured the tea, "because you knew. And you're our ancestor. And, on your deathbed, after the long and happy life with Zoe you're so determined not to have, you told us in case we ever needed it."

"And we needed it," Weldon adds.

"So we went and got it," Smantha adds. I'd like to say 'finishes,' but there's patently more to come, and true to form, Weldon continues, "and then we planted it and set it."

"You what?" I ask politely, mouth half-full of crumpet.

"We set the bomb," Weldon spells out.

"When?"

"Now." And he doesn't mean now-this-instant-now, of course. He means that Now is what the bomb is set to explode. *This* Now, the one I live in. The trailing edge of tranquil time I found at the edge of the devastation the war left. The near end of the rest of time, that's gone rolling peacefully away into the future from this point.

They're going to blow it all up. They're going to destroy the farm, the house, the fields, the robots, all my hard work. Turn it into a glittering desert of pulverised time. Like it had never been.

"But... why?" I croak, half a crumpet cooling on my plate.

"Because if they break the chain of causality so that their *Now* is the near edge of the rest of history, it doesn't matter what we do," Zoe says flatly. "We don't need to get together. It's a Causality Bomb. And they need to murder Causality to stay living. They've given up on us."

I leap up. "Where is it?"

"We're not going to tell you, of course," Weldon says implacably. "And we really should be going. Thanks for the tea."

I am outraged. I am outmanoeuvred. I am betrayed. I give Weldon and Smantha an agonised stare and cry out, "But I thought you were twee!"

They look at me, perfect eyes in perfect, perfect faces. "You have no idea," they say, "what we have done to protect our tweeness. You cannot imagine the sacrifices we have made, the elements of society we have expunged, the differences we have ruthlessly exterminated, so that we can live cosy, untroubled lives in our perfect world. And when we go back, we'll erase the memories from our minds so that we don't have to know either, and we can go about our pleasant, banal existence utterly untroubled by the mountain of bones we've built it all on." And all of this with only a modicum of feeling or expression, but then Smantha's face twists and she adds, "And all you had to do, to avoid this, was just settle down and have kids. Was that really so terrible? I swear, Weldon, ancestors these days just don't appreciate how hard we had it in the future."

For his part, Weldon ostentatiously checks a watch he has no real need to wear.

And then they're out and strolling towards their own time machine and gone.

"We need to find the bomb," Zoe says, but I know it doesn't matter. They won't have put it in the barn or the undercellar or wired it to the ignition of the Soviet Speedster. They're not dime novel villains. It's a Causality Bomb. The effective blast radius is the entire universe, all of space for that moment of time. And more than that, I know it goes off. That's why I've been feeling this sense of fragility to everything. It's the aftershock of the explosion, receding back in time. We're already living in a broken shard of time.

Which doesn't mean we won't get obliterated when the boom goes up.

We run. I don't know if running helps, but it seems wrong

to just saunter. I spend one vital second hugging Miffly goodbye because there's no way I can save her. We get in our time machines and exchange hurried coordinates. Rendezvous at the court of the Medicis in 1613 and take it from there. It's a decent length shard and there's some good Italian food.

And we won't take this lying down. We'll fight them every step of the way. And they'll hunt us, for sure. They'll track us through all the fragments of time and try to exterminate us, just as I did with the other survivors of the war. They'll set the same alarms I did, and jump on any intrusion to their perfect world. They'll make their own bottleneck and murder the crap out of any time traveller who gets that far, but most of all they will actively hunt us across infinity. Because we're two vengeful bastards with time machines, and we can still disrupt their precious Utopia. And we will. I swear that we will undo them. They'll wish they'd never been born.

But that's for tomorrow. Right now we have a more pressing problem.

WE GET OUT. The bomb goes off. The rest is history.